I0621191

The Enchanted Princess Wakes

Mary Catelli

Published by Wizard's Wood Press, 2025.

This is a work of fiction. Similarities to real people, places, or events are entirely coincidental.

THE ENCHANTED PRINCESS WAKES

First edition. April 3, 2025.

Copyright © 2025 Mary Catelli.

ISBN: 978-1-942564-73-7

Written by Mary Catelli.

Part I

The falls splashed off to one side, softly this late in summer, and the pine trees grew thickly about, muffling the sound. Here at her pool, ferns crowded to the brink of the perfectly circular and perfectly still pool. In the quiet, it showed a far distant scene.

The Fairy of the Pine Tree Falls knelt among the ferns to study it. A king and queen might enjoy a fine banquet, with every delicious item they could have cooked or roasted, baked or brewed, but the guests who enjoyed this feast were uncommon.

Indeed, one would expect them only at christenings.

A golden cloud of sparkles arose about one fairy. As if they were not dazzling enough in their finery. Then, the royalty and nobility gleamed in gold, jewels, and silk. To outdo them, fairies had to do what they could not. Giving gifts to the child was not enough.

If you could call them gifts. Sometimes you could, to be sure.

A fairy laughed, but all she heard, of course, was the light splashing of the falls.

Her gaze went over the guests. They had not invited her. She breathed deeply. The scent of pine was calming, but this was no time for peace.

Her eyes narrowed, and she dismissed the enchantment. Once again the pool showed only the reflections of pines and ferns, and she did not look on them. Someone had machinations in play. They were likely to be perilous for the mountain kingdom and its subjects, and might be for the princess.

She stood and shook out her skirt. It was better when you disguised yourself as an old woman and took offense at the rude princes and princesses, and rewarded the courteous, but when the other fairies became godmothers, she had no choice if she wanted the land to be safe. Fortunately, it was known that fairies took offense at not being invited to christenings as godmothers.

\#

As she swept down the castle path, past late blooming roses, the banqueting hall came into a view. A sweet voice rose from it. They had already started the gifts, she could not count and know that she arrived after all the others had given theirs. Though the Fairy of Golden Waterlily Lake gave her gift now, still, others might have before her.

She had to curse wisely. Wisely enough that if every other fairy gave after, they could not undo it.

Up the stairs and through the door, and into the gathering.

Everyone at court had worn their finest. Gold and rubies, and silk and pearls, were everywhere. The Fairy of Pine Tree Falls smiled sourly and pressed forward. It took many courtiers a moment to realize that she did not glitter and gleam and yet was not a servant. They parted enough for her to approach the crib.

There, the queen saw her, and started.

If you wanted me in greens as brilliant as emeralds and beryls, thought the Fairy of Pine Tree Falls, you should have invited me. Nothing like having me appear in dark shades to warn that I noticed the insult.

The other, invited fairies had not stinted on colors, looking as brilliant as wildflowers in a summer meadow.

Neither had the royalty. Her eyes narrowed as she looked at the guests in royal scarlet, adorned with gold. King Henry. His son Prince Henry, young for these events, but still looking sour. They must have sent many couriers back and forth discussing this, and King Henry must have great intentions for this visit. He would never visit for less, and to bring his son as well meant even more.

A royal match. King Henry had to believe that Princess Rosaleen would inherit the throne. And such a match would mean only trouble for the lands all about.

She had come to give the innocent princess a christening gift, she reminded herself. Perhaps the only innocent in the room. She walked forward. The other fairies were already rustling and whispering among themselves.

It was just as well she had not stopped to change her clothes. To sweep up in dark green and blue, without a bit of jewelry, underscored her wrath, and she had the time to think, and even to compose her face into a mask of calm.

Rosaleen cooed.

From the corner of the rooms, soldiers moved, recognizable by their blue coats. For a moment, she fancied that they were clockwork soldiers, fantastical in nature and capable of acting perfectly as long as they were wound up, but their pale, sweating faces showed they were men. And courageous ones, she conceded, if perhaps foolish.

King Ian gestured to them, and they paused. Obedient soldiers, and a prudent king.

She walked forward with measured pace. Even the other fairies could not act until she did. They knew the weakness of their enchantments when they had failed to invite her.

The Fairy of Pine Tree Falls looked down into the cradle, and the princess looked back. She would have green eyes, the fairy thought. And, no doubt, be beautiful, since that was always the first gift.

All about her, silence reigned.

She drew out her wand and waved it. Dark violet and dark blue hung in the air over the cradle.

"You, o Princess Rosaleen, will fall into an enchanted sleep before you turn eighteen, and from it you will only awaken from the kiss of a prince whom you will marry, and you twain shall live happily ever after."

Rosaleen cooed again. The silence, if anything, was deeper after that. The Fairy of Pine Tree Falls looked up and about the glittering hall. The soldiers looked relieved—the courtiers, less so—and both kings and Prince Henry, furious.

Being, thought the Fairy of Pine Tree Falls, already aware that Prince Henry could never make his bride happy.

The other fairies were clustered together in silence, as if whispering would betray their plots.

One stepped forward. The Fairy of Cherry Blossom Hill, all delicate in pink, her wand in hand, left the group and drew all gazes. Her face was calm enough.

The Fairy of Pine Trees Falls kept her own face equally calm, even placid, but she could not keep her breath from catching. She had not had days and weeks and months to ponder the significance of her gift, which meant that whatever flaw this fairy found in her gift—or curse—would not astound her. There was always a flaw.

The Fairy of Cherry Blossom Hill waved her wand over the cradle. Pink sparks flew.

"She will not wake while the prince is there, and not until a month and a day after he leaves, and she will not sleep alone, the castle will fall asleep about her, and—"

A fairy in blue kicked her in the ankle, and with a startled cry, the Fairy of Cherry Blossom Hill fell silent. The Fairy of Pine Tree Falls let her breath out and hoped that her relief did not show. Nothing in that gift would harm the princess, or, for that matter, the prince.

Moments inched by. Her gaze went over the set faces. Many were growing pale. King Henry's was growing red. Slowly, it dawned on her that the Fairy of Cherry Blossom Hill had been the last. They could not put forth another fairy to foil her.

The Fairy of Sapphire Bay did not look pleased. Neither did the others.

Then, they wouldn't, thought the Fairy of Pine Tree Falls. She turned and swept from the room. The crowd opened much more easily this time.

"You idiot," whispered one fairy, when the Fairy of Pine Tree Falls had not quite escaped earshot, "were you trying to put the kingdom asleep?"

That would have improved the matter, thought the Fairy of Pine Tree Falls. No amount of diplomacy would alleviate that, and King Henry, or Prince Henry, could do little to the kingdom while it slept. Alas, it would not be.

Sunlight shone over the late roses, blooming in deep red before her, and all abuzz with bees. Princess Rosaleen would just have to manage with no more than the castle.

Part II

A side room in the castle, where commonly the scribes worked, indeed held a scribe, scribbling at a desk by such daylight as the cloudy sky gave through the windows. Also a few grave officials, and the king.

The huntsmen bowed. Their leader straightened and remembered the courtesy drummed into him. King Ian must speak first.

"Ah, Ronald Greenlane," he said. "Have my commands been fulfilled?"

Reynold Greenleaf said, "The castle is ready for Her Royal Highness." And held his tongue that it was, in truth, a small castle that King Jehan used for a hunting lodge. No doubt the king knew that. And if he did not, it did not matter in the slightest.

King Ian nodded. "It will do. Take my daughter with all speed." He waved at a doorway where a lady with graying hair held a tiny child who stared about, and a maidservant wrung her hands. Both women were dressed for travel.

"I will send more servants as needed."

Reynold started to reckon. At least a cook and a washing woman. With the child so young, little more would be needed, for a time. They would be fortunate to gain more, though. The king and queen could forget the princess more easily with her in the mountains—and her newborn brother with them.

He bowed again and gestured for the women to follow before the hair-splitting retreat from the room without turning his back on the king. As if anyone would want to.

Grooms already readied the horses, including the gentle nags that looked ready to hold the lady and the child, and the maidservant. He eyed the clouds.

David said, "There's a place we can stop within an hour, if we make good time." He eyed the nags. The lady spoke with the nursemaid in a low voice.

6

"The sooner we leave," said Reynold, "the better time it will be."

#

After the rain, and the mud the next days, they had traveled swiftly enough.

With her nag moving easily enough along the path, however narrow, Gilliane looked up at the mountains. The birches, white as snow, had enough of a gap that she could see the peaks, some of which did not have trees. They were deep in the mountains. She had known companies with nobles and even royalty that did not move so swiftly.

The breeze rustled the leaves and tugged at her sleeve.

"So much cooler here," said Gilliane.

The huntsmen did not speak. Even Reynold merely nodded. Then, they knew that winter was coming. So did she, but it had been years since she had lived in the mountains.

The sunlight turned green by passing through birch leaves and fell on the road. Princess Rosaleen chortled and waved her arms. The maidservant Kate kept her grip as they went around another bend, this one about a rocky slope. Beyond, the mountainside fell, and they could see the whole valley. The village stood ahead, close enough that Gilliane could see the villagers peering at the company. The castle stood a little back, half-hidden by the trees. Her eyebrows went up. She had known it was barely a castle, but she had never before seen a castle less prominent than the village.

Voices echoed, oddly clear. Someone asked if it were true that the queen had borne a son.

Princess Rosaleen crowed and leaned forward, toward some wildflowers growing in the ditch. Gilliane's mouth drew into a line. It was, of course, true. Princess Rosaleen had to be exiled to a place—any place—where she could not put her brother to sleep.

Gilliane forced her breath out. King Ian justly did not want Prince Giovanni to sleep. Had the fairies given the prince some protection against the curse, at his christening, perhaps the princess could have stayed at her father's castle. But she, and all the rest, had listened so attentively to each fairy and heard nothing.

Perhaps the Fairy of Cherry Blossom Hill had not found adding her curse to that of the Fairy of Pine Tree Falls enough, and they had refrained for fear of thwarting her.

Princess Rosaleen grabbed at a red blossom.

Even though they had taken care that the Fairy of Cherry Blossom Hill had gone first.

She looked back at the village. Many villagers had come out to gawk, it seemed.

Reynold cleared his throat. "We can shout over to them. Getting there's a bit more of a bear."

Princess Rosaleen grumbled at the petals in her fingers.

#

In all this journey, they had never arrived so late at their destination. Gilliane tried again and again to reckon the road, but then a new twist would render all her guesses moot. Princess Rosaleen grew truly fretful in the last hours, as the sky turned fiery red. Then, as it darkened, she started to nod in Kate's arms.

The moon rose, a sullen orange, but the twists of the road meant the mountains and trees often blocked it from view even as it rose, and paled through yellow to white.

When Kate yawned, Reynold took Rosaleen from her arms, and let the princess rest against his chest. As they rode the last stretch—the road went to the castle, not the village—servants emerged with lanterns, to Gilliane's relief. Moonlight might, perhaps, have sufficed, but the dancing orange torchlight, for all the shadows it cast, brightened the way.

Grooms came to take horses, Reynold came to give the sleeping princess into her arms, and maids led her and Kate to the crib already

ready, so that Rosaleen could just be laid down and covered with a blanket. She slept there as if she were already under the cursed sleep. Gilliane let out her breath. The maid had pointed out their rooms, of course, but the bustle of the arrival left her tired, indeed, but not ready for sleep.

Kate sat.

"I will look about," said Gilliane, taking up a candle.

Kate shrugged and did not say she would find nothing out of the ordinary.

Gilliane, suspecting she would find nothing out of the ordinary, looked about. The corridors, if not long compared to the palace's, were still long enough by candlelight. The servants answered frankly whenever she spoke to them. None of them pulled back, or fled from her sight. They were fortunate to get the princess, thought Gilliane, who had not yet grown accustomed to court. The king and queen would expect to be served as if by invisible hands.

Then, were the king and queen to come here, they would have brought their own servants and not been content with peasants hired on the mountain.

She tried a door. It opened on a library.

She blinked. Shelves of books. Not so many as in the castle where the king and queen—and little prince—lived now, but more than she had ever seen in a lord's home.

She bit her lip. A governess would find it useful, if they ever sent one. Slowly, she walked in and looked about as the shadows and candlelight played over the shelves. If.

She told herself not to be a fool. They would think a just punishment of the prince the fairy had promised, that his bride, however happy she made him, was ill-educated to be a queen.

She drew in her breath and let it out again. At the very least, she could teach Rosaleen her letters.

She could teach her dancing as well. Teaching her how to manage a household, with this hunting lodge being all that she knew, would be more difficult.

#

In great swathes along the mountainside, leaves had turned golden. Some of the green trees were pine and fir, Gilliane noted. Behind her, Rosaleen squealed as she ran in the garden, not caring about the want of flowers.

Footsteps sounded on the path behind her, and she turned. Reynold Greenleaf had his cap off, and he bowed.

"News, my lady. It's about Kate."

Gilliane blinked. She had seen little of Kate even since they arrived. The mountain girls had done more of the nursery work.

He cleared his throat. "She ran off. The other servants wondered if she had gotten lost, but a lad saw her go. With the last merchants."

Gilliane's breath gusted out. "Well. May God speed her journey."

Reynold hesitated. "Should we send word to the king?"

"We have nursemaids enough here. What good would it do?" She spread her hands. "If fall frightened her, what would winter do to the one who came after?"

Reynold snorted.

#

Snow swirled about outside the window in a manner that three years had made familiar, and Rosaleen danced about the room in her shift. Her steps would not, thought Gilliane, pass muster in a ballroom, but they kept her out of the hands of her nursemaid.

She bounced up on her toes before a dresser, and peered into the mirror there. "Mirror, mirror, on the wall! Who's the fairest of them all?"

Then she squeaked, "Look, it's me!"

The nursemaid rolled her eyes.

"It doesn't do to listen to half the lesson," said Gilliane.

"Story!" squealed Rosaleen and ran across the room to Gilliane.

"Once you know how to read," said Gilliane, "you will be able to read whenever you wish. You could read, for yourself, all the stories."

Rosaleen looked brightly up at her. "Story!"

#

Lady Gilliane walked briskly into the brilliant sunlight. Rosaleen scurried after. A princess who had to walk to the next kingdom would not stand about. Still less one who might have to walk past thrice ten kingdoms.

They walked into the cool shade, and then the sunlight broke in again, on a spread of grass where a peasant woman greeted Lady Gilliane, and half a dozen little girls turned to look at the princess.

Rosaleen looked back.

"Why do you sit all those hours in the room with all those books?" said one of the younger ones, and one of the others whispered, "Briony!"

"I'm supposed to learn all the stories," said Rosaleen.

An older girl's nose wrinkled. "How many are there?"

"Lots and lots!" Rosaleen's arms threw out to either side. "I learned about Maid Maleen today."

"Who's Maid Maleen?" said Briony.

"She was a princess," said Rosaleen. "Like me."

"Then she's be Princess Maleen," said a boy, sullenly.

"The story called her Maid," said Rosaleen.

The boy opened his mouth, and Lady Gilliane said, firmly, "You hinder the princess in her tale. And thus hearing how she came to be called that."

The boy pouted, and Rosaleen looked at the girls before going on.

"But she and a prince wanted to marry each other, and her father didn't want her to marry him.

"So-o-o—" She spread her arms. "He locked her in a tower with a maidservant and food for seven years, to teach her a lesson. But when the years were nearly up, Maleen realized that no one was chiseling at the tower to get them out again. So she and the maidservant pried their way out."

"How?" said one girl, her nose wrinkling.

"Stuff they had about." Rosaleen waved her hands about and tried not to scowl. They *had* gotten out, so there must have been something.

"That wouldn't work well," said one older girl, red-haired.

"Why didn't they do it earlier?" said a third.

"Because," said the red-haired girl, "it would just make her father mad."

Rosaleen shrugged. "They got out. And when they got out, no one was there. All the land was laid waste by war. They had to leave the kingdom entirely, and they ate thistles on the way. Raw."

The appalled looks from the girls made her hesitate, but she went on.

"They got to the kingdom of the prince who had wanted to marry her, and they looked for work. They finally got to work as maids at the royal castle. But the prince had accepted his father's plea to marry, because he thought Maid Maleen was dead."

Some girls grimaced at that.

"So, his bride arrived, but she was very ugly, and she told Maid Maleen that she had to take her place at the wedding, so that no one would see how ugly she was." Rosaleen lowered her voice. "She didn't say that. She said it was because she sprained her ankle."

The girls giggled.

"So Maid Maleen put on the wedding gown and went, and the prince thought that if he had not known his beloved had died in the war in her father's lands, he would have thought that the bride was Maid Maleen. But he took her by the hand and led her to the church.

"On the path there, a thistle plant grew, and she murmured that once she had eaten it unbroiled, and she had eaten it unroasted, and the prince asked what she said, and she said she was thinking of Maid Maleen. Then they came to a bridge and she murmured, asking it to not break, she was not the true bride. The prince asked her what she said, and she said she was thinking of Maid Maleen. Then they came to the church door, and she murmured, asking it to not break, she was not the true bride. The prince asked her what she said, and she said she was thinking of Maid Maleen.

"So, they married. Maid Maleen went back to the bride, and the bride came out, veiled, for the wedding feast, but the prince questioned her about what she had said, and she had to go back to Maid Maleen to find out. Finally, she was so afraid that the prince would find out that she ordered Maid Maleen killed, and the prince found out. So he had *her* head cut off, and he married Maid Maleen."

Girls nodded, or smiled, or objected that he had already married her.

"If," said Briony, "she had just let Maid Maleen take her place forever, there wouldn't have been a problem. They wouldn't have cut her head off."

"Would they?" said a little girl.

"Oh no," said Rosaleen. "Sometimes the first bride gets there in the nick of time, and they don't cut off the head of the second bride. Sometimes she gets to marry someone else."

The little girl scowled.

"I think, Briony," said the tallest girl, brown-haired, "that it was more than she tried to kill Maid Maleen." A chorus of voices rose in discussion of it. One said that she couldn't have been a princess, or the king would have been angry.

"He's lucky he didn't marry her, she was probably part ogre," said the red-haired girl, and the other girls rolled their eyes, and one said, "An ogre wouldn't let them cut her head off, Polly."

"We didn't come here to tell stories," said one of the oldest girls.

"Really?" said Rosaleen.

"She's right," said Polly, confidingly. "Our mothers wanted us out of the way while they made soap."

The other girl looked sullen. "We could just sit in the corner and tell stories down there. But up here, there's the grass."

Rosaleen blinked. Yes, here there was a lawn.

"We came here to play Sally Go Round the Sun," said Briony, brightly.

"How do you play that?" said Rosaleen.

"Haven't you played Sally Go Round The Sun?" said Briony.

"We all join hands in a circle," said Polly, and they did. "Then we go about in a circle while we sing."

"And we go faster all the time!" said the sullen girl, brightening up.

"Until we fall down!" said a boy.

"We know that, Mat," said Polly.

"Does she?" He pointed at Rosaleen.

"I know now," said Rosaleen, and they all laughed.

So they ran, and they sang, "Sally go round the sun, Sally go round the moon, Sally go round the stars, on a Sunday afternoon," over and over, until one tripped, and all tumbled, laughing.

And looked up to see they were watched, by Lady Gilliane, who looked serene, and by the peasant woman, looking shocked.

"You could have knocked out the princess's teeth!"

"Playing Sally Go Round the Sun?" said Lady Gilliane, mildly. "I played that many times as a girl. Do you play it rougher here?" She looked at the girls. "How many of you have knocked your teeth out?"

The peasant woman's breath was drawn in sharply. "The princess can not play with peasants!"

Lady Gilliane shrugged. "Little princes and princesses play with servant children until they are old enough to get their own households. And the royal castle hires peasants like anyone else."

"Well," said the woman, "perhaps they should not play Sally Go Round The Sun again."

Briony stood up. "We could go play Maid Maleen! Polly gets to be Maid Maleen! And Mat gets to be the prince!"

#

Stars appeared over the sunset as they walked back.

"It's all very well to play Sally Go Round the Sun," said Lady Gilliane. "But it's not a proper dance even among peasants. You should have proper dancing lessons. Not all princesses are lucky enough to be sent to the wedding in the bride's place. Some have to go to three dances to break a spell on the prince's memory."

Rosaleen kept watching the path. Some tree roots could trip her. "Who would I dance with?"

"Peasants dance, too. Girls and boys need to learn. If any of your new friends run away from home and end up in a castle where they hold a dance so the prince can choose his bride, they will be able to dance at it."

Rosaleen giggled. "They need fine dresses to catch his eye."

"Perhaps they will," said Lady Gilliane. "You will need lessons more than they do."

Rosaleen nodded. Then she blinked. "Why did they call her Maid Maleen? The prince knew she was a princess!"

Lady Gilliane sighed. "Back in the day, they only called kings, kings. They didn't call their wives queens, but the king's wife. They didn't call their sons princes but king's sons."

Rosaleen yawned, but said, "And they didn't call their daughters princess but king's daughters."

"Even so. And when they were young and maids, they called them maids."

#

In the wan light, barely brighter than a candle, Rosaleen stared at the map, where waterfalls were scattered, dry as a bone on the paper. She wished for the days when she learned about Maid Maleen and not what it took to get to the prince's kingdom, and sat back.

The window was a bleary mess of drab color. Outside, torrents hammered on the roof and flooded off in waterfalls of their own. Even dancing lessons could be tedious, but she wondered if geography could ever be interesting. Idly, she glanced over the place names.

"We should go on a pilgrimage," she said.

Lady Gilliane looked over from her reading.

"There." She pointed at the chapel of Saint Gualberto. "It would serve as a pious undertaking." And would take us past several waterfalls, she thought.

Lady Gilliane looked at the map. "I could send word to court that it's to pray for your parents and brothers, they would not object to that."

Rosaleen looked at the map. Messages to court. Always so tedious and took so long. And so arbitrary when they came back.

Then Lady Gilliane frowned. "I would have to arrange a company. Villagers would be needed, or foresters. And we have to go at a time when they will be able to leave. No harvest or planting." She glanced at her. "You do know that when they are doing those, they will stay up as long as there is moonlight to work by."

Rosaleen bit her lip. Lady Gilliane knew she knew. She and the peasant children could not play Maid Maleen, or Kate Crackernuts, or the Snake Prince at either time.

Lady Gilliane looked out the window as if she could see something, and she mused rather than spoke. "Then, they often have gone on pilgrimage. Some might leap at the chance, not to be the odd ones out."

A gust of wind rattled the windows, but hope burned for her. Her heart pattering, Rosaleen looked back at the map. She would pray for the village and for the prince who was supposed to rescue her. And she would learn how to travel on roads in the mountains. She needed to know that, for after the curse broke.

She smiled radiantly at the map, and began to trace the routes out of the mountains, since a prince had to come from another kingdom.

Forest, fields, rivers, hills, marsh, and more mountains. Rosaleen scowled and pulled the map closer to the lamp. Better lighting did not make those marks make more sense. They looked like waves on land, and the sea was nearby. "What are those? Is that where the tide comes in?"

"Those," said Lady Gilliane, "are sand dunes. They can spread over your path." She pulled the map back. "You will not go on pilgrimage there."

"The prince might be past them. After he wakes me up. If he came from there."

"Then you should take a ship."

#

They had planted rosemary outside the window, that was supposed to do something for remembering what she studied, and Rosaleen sat with the book open before her. A history.

Lady Gilliane spoke in a low voice outside the library door. The woman with her was not so soft-spoken.

"Three healthy sons is a fine crop. It's a pity about the princess, but it would be worse if she were the only one. And if there were two more princesses, King Henry still might be angry about the failed match."

"When would he not be angry?" said Lady Gilliane, mildly.

Rosaleen let her breath out in a huff. Always talking about King Henry, and never telling her. They would fall silent when they realized that she was near, but she knew it had *something* to do with the curse.

The gentlemen her father had sent to manage her household (with Lady Gilliane muttering about how the king might have managed men of lower birth if he really tried) were the worst. Though this woman sounded as bad.

Lady Gilliane spoke on. "Nor does it matter here. If your ride was not so onerous that you must rest, it is time for you to meet the princess."

Rosaleen looked back at the book and pretended to read as the door opened, and light fell over the page, with the shadows of women.

"Rosaleen, your parents have sent a new attendant."

She looked over.

The lady curtsied. Which was not like the curtsies of the country women, any more than their menfolk bowed like courtiers. She supposed the lady would say it was only proper that the peasants did not ape their betters. But the lady was already straightening, and she had to rise from her seat so that Lady Cynthia could be presented to her.

"She studies in this library," said Lady Gilliane.

"It is—large," said Lady Cynthia.

"It's because of Queen Katherine!" said Rosaleen, and caught how startled Lady Gilliane looked. She had wondered when Rosaleen had asked her. Now— "I just read it. King Jehan loved to hunt, so Queen Katherine had a library put here so she could read."

Lady Gilliane smiled and came into the room, looking over Rosaleen's shoulder at the book. Lady Cynthia looked appalled.

Lady Gilliane murmured, "I hope she likes to embroider." Rosaleen glanced at her. She nodded at Lady Cynthia. Then, she knew Rosaleen's embroidery was—adequate.

The church bells chimed, down in the village, and Rosaleen said, "Now I should go for my walk."

Lady Cynthia agreed with great alacrity. As they donned their hats against the sun, Rosaleen said, "I read about giants, too, today."

"What did they do?" said Lady Gilliane.

"A prince found them when he was on a journey."

They started down the corridor.

"He had met a beautiful princess who turned into a dove, but an evil old witch bewitched him to sleep when they were going to meet again. He had to go after her, and he met two giants. They were thieves and fighting over how to divide up what they had stolen: a pair of boots that would take you anywhere, a cap to make you invisible, and a bugle that would summon an army. He told them that he would judge for them, but first he had to make sure that they worked.

"He slapped on the cap, pulled on the boots, and strode off to the dove princess's land. The evil old witch was making her marry the witch's son, but the prince blew on the bugle, and that was the end of that."

She twirled about. "It's going to be fun. We'll have to say that the other side of the village is the new kingdom, and everyone's going to have to run to get ahead of him." Lady Cynthia eyed her. "Whoever plays him," she explained.

"She plays with the peasant children?" said Lady Cynthia. "At her age?"

"You are free to write to Their Majesties on the matter," said Lady Gilliane, and Lady Cynthia opened her mouth, shut it again, and walked along the corridor, looking resentful.

Lady Gilliane opened the door, and a warm breeze bore in the scent of roses. For a moment, Lady Cynthia looked content.

Bees bumbled from rose to rose as they walked down the hedges of roses. Rosaleen pointed out this flower and that and told how some had been planted. Lady Cynthia listened with gravity and asked a few questions about the plants in sheltered corners, carefully facing south.

They came out on a hillside. Below, in the sunshine, spread the village and its fields, and to either hand the forest stood. The slopes held pine stands in places, but here the woods were thick with maple and beech.

"Now," said Rosaleen, "we walk for a bit in the forest."

"I don't see a path," said Lady Cynthia.

"Oh, we don't go that far. If the lodge is in sight, we can still come back. Besides, the forest means the trees cast shade. No sunlight, and it's cooler here."

Silence lasted a moment.

Rosaleen skipped ahead. Dead leaves crunched underfoot. "Sometimes we go up to the pines, and birches, but we can get a huntsman to come with us then, if you don't know the way. I can get to the birches all on my own!" She twirled about a beech and grinned. "Once we went up the mountains, and to the chapel of Saint Gualberto—a pilgrimage. With an escort, because it was too far to be found by a huntsman."

Silence lasted several moments. No breeze ruffled the branches.

"What a wretched place this is," muttered Lady Cynthia. Rosaleen blinked. Lady Cynthia didn't seem to notice her attention. Maybe she had thought she had been quiet enough. She calmly turned to Lady Gilliane.

"What if we fell and were injured?" said Lady Cynthia.

"The grooms in the stable," said Lady Gilliane. "The gentlemen of chamber. The huntsmen of the forest. It would not be difficult to be brought back to the lodge. Easier than from some distant parts of the royal castle where the king lives, untroubled."

"But that would be bad because there is dancing tonight." Rosaleen laughed. "I am good at country dances."

Lady Cynthia's face set in lines like a mask.

Rosaleen skipped. "I get to do some of the dances, for the girls and boys, but not for all that long. We have to go to bed."

Lady Cynthia murmured about how long a journey it had been, how many days it had taken, how weary she was, whether she would be lively enough to attend dancing.

Lady Gilliane said, quickly, "All the gentlemen of her household attend."

Lady Cynthia straightened at that, and looked happier.

#

Snowflakes gently floated by the window, adding to the snow that had already covered the rose bushes in the garden. The dried stands of flowers had long vanished beneath it.

Her ladies, accumulated over the years, sat as far as they could from the windows and embroidered together, exclaiming over how early the snow came.

Rosaleen pulled back from the window. The heaviness was one thing, but the earliness was not, in fact, that out of the ordinary. She headed out the door, into the dim corridor, glad that she could plead her studies and go to the library.

Though, at the moment, there was only one question of history she wanted answered, and she could not study for it there. Perhaps it had not even been written in a book yet.

The library's doorway stood, bright with daylight, ahead of her.

The ladies might be able to answer. That was, they might know the answer. But she thought of their exclamations and their laughter at the question and its bluntness, and how it showed that she had never been at court. One or two of the ladies might fish around, delicately, if asked when alone, but Rosaleen felt coldly certain they would, in their mirth or delicacy, either overlook her question entirely or hide that they thought that she had been kept ignorant by intent, which they would not question.

She walked through the doorway. Lady Gilliane, with her book, sat in the gray light by the window, despite the cold, and nodded to her without looking up much.

Rosaleen swallowed, and said, "What was the problem with the curse at my christening?"

Lady Gilliane started, and then stared at her.

Now that she asked, the questions flooded out. "Princesses have had to sleep before. She didn't even make me sleep for a hundred years. Why did that make King Henry so angry? And my parents, too? Why did they send me up here? Why are all my gentlemen never nobles, and all my ladies orphans?"

Lady Gilliane sighed, slowly. She marked where she read and closed the book, and turned to face Rosaleen.

"The problem turned on your being the heir to your father."

"I have brothers," said Rosaleen.

"You have brothers—now," said Lady Gilliane. "Then, you could have married Prince Henry and united the kingdoms." She fell silent.

Rosaleen scowled in thought. "He's a prince. He could have woken me up. Could still wake me up."

"No," said Lady Gilliane. "He could not have. That was the part with how you would live happily with your husband." Her tongue touched her lips. "You might have lived in contentment as queen, but even at that age, everyone knew that Prince Henry would not make his bride happy."

"Really?"

"And if anyone had doubted, the years have only confirmed it." Lady Gilliane sighed. "King Henry raged and insisted that your parents had arranged it, had given their word. You might have been queen of a vast realm as his son's bride, but they had foiled it for you."

Rosaleen blinked.

Lady Gilliane plowed on. "King Henry might see to it. A vast realm at any rate. You read the tale of Maid Maleen, every child in the village can attest to that."

"She was locked in a tower," said Rosaleen, slowly, wondering what that tale had to do with it, "and while she was—" Her eyes widened as she realized. An army had ravaged the kingdom. "Did she ever learn what had happened to her father?" But he must have died, she thought. Otherwise, he would have done something when his daughter married the prince, if no earlier.

Lady Gilliane watched her.

"I would have refused," said Rosaleen. "I don't have to marry him. I could run away and become a scullery maid and marry the prince there after I went to the ball three times."

Lady Gilliane raised an eyebrow.

"Not if he would ravage the country!"

"The point," said Lady Gilliane dryly, "of arranging a marriage is to join the countries without a war ravaging the country."

"Not if he fought a dragon!"

"That might be wise." Lady Gilliane sat back. "The Fairy of the Pine Tree Falls said that you would fall asleep, and be woken by a prince who would marry you, and you would live happily ever after. No one believes that Prince Henry would make you happy. At all."

Rosaleen pondered that. The wind blew against the windows. She sat. "Why did the other fairy say that I would not wake up until the prince was long gone?"

Lady Gilliane sighed. The wind was still, for once, and Rosaleen wondered if Lady Gilliane would keep the secret as well as the other ladies. Snow sifted by the window.

"Everyone knows," said Lady Gilliane, slowly, "that the fairy who is not invited curses the child, and that a curse is evil, and that it must be undone as best it can be. Apparently the Fairy of Cherry Blossom Hill thought that would undo it as far as it could be done."

Rosaleen scowled.

Lady Gilliane smiled wryly. "That is why your parents sent you away. They will govern the land, and then perhaps your brother will, and perhaps even his grandson, and you will sleep, and the prince will wake you, and you will chase after him and marry him live in his kingdom. Happily ever after for everyone, no doubt."

Rosaleen sat back. "Perhaps even his great-great-grandson." Snow blew onto the window, with soft splatters. "Perhaps they will suggest his great-great-grandson marry my great-great-granddaughter because I slept only seven years."

Lady Gillian snorted. "Or three days. She set no lower limit, either."

#

A breeze from the orchards threw loose petals through the air.

In the grass between the orchard and the castle, a girl dressed in green towered over a kneeling girl, as the kneeling girl said, "Oh Queen of the Snakes, please give me back my husband!" About her, the other children hissed.

Gilliane smiled a little. Neither the queen nor the other snakes looked at all serpentine, and the queen certainly did not have the three heads of the tale, but at least the children enjoyed it.

Then, the tale was coming to an end.

She turned away from the window. No, thought Gilliane, at least it encouraged Rosaleen in her studies. She started down the corridor. The king should have sent Princess Rosaleen a proper governess. One thing to watch the child learn to walk, or to teach her her letters, but now she had to read as earnestly as she could to keep ahead of her charge. If Rosaleen loved to read, she might have set her loose, but except for tales that she could tell the other children, Rosaleen was dutiful enough, and no more—Gilliane scowled. She had little confidence that she taught her all she needed to know. She still sometimes had to read by candlelight to master the lesson she wanted to teach the next day.

Could any princess be properly taught from this library? She had not gained more books any more than she had gained a governess. Did they never think of what would happened when their son, or grandson, or great-grandson, had to treat with the kingdom where Rosaleen was the crown prince's bride?

A gaggle of ladies stood in the corridor, talking solemnly. Only three of them, and Gilliane frowned. Where was Lady Cynthia?

"And with Master Duncan!" exclaimed Lady Francesca. She turned. "Did you hear, Lady Gilliane? Lady Cynthia ran off with Master Duncan!"

"No, no, I had not." Gilliane wondered a little that it had taken so long. She had met the man at the dances in the village—all those who worked at the castle went—and then there was only the matter of their escape.

Lady Francesca spread her hands. "I wonder what they were thinking—both of them with no family and no friends."

Gilliane smiled coolly. After the curse fell, none of them would have family or friends, even if it lasted only a year and a day, as all of them were orphans without connections to escape this lodge.

And none of the ladies were actual help with the princess.

"Let us hope they are fortunate enough not to be cursed for Master Duncan to forget her," she said. "I doubt Lady Cynthia could remind him of her so as to break to spell."

The ladies tittered. Gilliane managed a smile. She wondered if these three would linger as long as Lady Cynthia had. She went by, into the library, and they gossiped on as she started to organize the books. The number of books was enough, if they had been chosen with an eye to educating a princess suitable, as they had not been. She sighed and put down a book. She looked out, and her gaze took in the window.

Rosaleen stood outside it. As if she had started up the path—the peasant children had dispersed—and been distracted by—birds in a tree.

Better than staring at her reflection in the glass, Gilliane told herself, going to the door. "Lesson time," she called brightly.

Rosaleen started back up the path, but slowly, glancing back, and when she reached the door, she turned to Gilliane.

"What," said Rosaleen, dreamily, "if those birds are seven brothers turned into doves because their father cursed them in a moment of folly?"

"Definitely lesson time, if you forgot that those were ravens. The dove boys were caught when their sister foolishly picked rosemary from the grave of an ogre." She stepped back from the door, holding it open.

Rosaleen's nose wrinkled as she went in. "I wish I lived in the days when wishing still did some good."

"Foolish of you," said Gilliane. "Someone could wish you into a frog. Once upon a time, there was a girl so beautiful that she seemed to say, 'Sun, there is no need to shine, for I am shining.' Three princes saw her once, and started to quarrel over her. They made such a ruckus that a witch nearby cursed her into a frog for causing all that trouble, and the princes made up and went off, and the frog hopped off into a marsh."

Rosaleen looked at her so brightly that she realized she was trapped, and had to finish the tale. At least, she told herself, Rosaleen was not staring out the window.

"But a king nearby decided to choose between his three sons, which should be his heir. He sent them off to find brides, and told them to bring back linen shirts their brides had sewn. At a crossroads, the two older sons decreed they must part: they would go the well-traveled road to cities, and the youngest, the ill-kept up road into the marsh, or they would kill him. The youngest went, but the road went into the mud, and he bewailed his fate.

"The frog appeared and asked him what he needed. He told her, and she brought him the finest linen shirt, embroidered in blue and gold. He brought it back, and his brothers brought back theirs. The oldest son's, their father proclaimed was fit for one of his stable hands, the middle son's, fit to be worn on a fast day, the youngest son's, to be worn on the greatest of feasts.

"Then he sent them off to bring back bread baked by their brides, and the oldest son brought back a loaf fit only for dogs, the middle son, a loaf fit for servants on an ordinary day, and the youngest son, a loaf fit for the high table at the greatest of feasts.

"Then he told them that he would hold a ball, and they were to bring their brides to dance at it. The youngest was certain that now he would be shamed, but the frog told him to go himself and announce that she followed. When a coach arrived, he was to say that she was his bride.

"At the court, the older brothers produced their brides, who were graceful and beautiful and finely dressed, and jeered at him, but he said only that his bride was following. Then a servant ran in and declared that a coach of silver pulled by horses of gold was driving up. The youngest said, 'That is my bride.'

"The couch stopped before the castle and a girl emerged, so beautiful that she seemed to say to the Sun, 'Sun, there is no need to shine, for I am shining.'

"The prince went to her and said she was his bride. They went into the dance, and no one in the hall could dance as two of them did. The king choose him for his heir."

Rosaleen sat back from the window. "She did marry a prince."

Gilliane fought down a sigh. It would only make Rosaleen more stubborn.

"You wouldn't marry a prince if you had to win him that way. You can not sew or bake well enough. Perhaps you could dance well enough, but it is not good enough to do one thing. Thus, wishes like that would do you no good."

Rosaleen pouted. Slowly, sullenly, she turned toward the door. Then she stared down the slope. "Why is that—"

Gilliane scowled. A messenger rode toward the castle. Her eyes narrowed. A messenger riding full speed. They had never had such a messenger, not since the first day Rosaleen arrived here. Not even the births of her two younger brothers had inspired them to send the news so swiftly.

And she had no hope of bring Rosaleen to her studies while she was so intent on the traveler.

She sighed. At least she could call for the news.

And listen in shock as the messenger said that King Henry had died.

#

Sunlight through the leaves dappled the ground, and all the youngsters in its patchy shade were intent on Giles, returned from a visit to town. He looked gleeful in his news. The lanky youth looked about the circle of children from toddlers who did not understand to those almost full grown. Rosaleen bit her lip.

"Prince Henry," said Giles, "brought King Henry a beautiful princess with magical powers to marry, and the princess said she couldn't marry so old and ugly a king, and made a fire for him to jump through to fix that, but he made Prince Henry jump first, and now he's handsome, but then the king jumped through and it worked for only one so he was all burned up."

Rosaleen frowned. "But—why would he bring back a princess for his father? A *stepmother*? That ends badly. He could have been turned into a crow!"

"Well," said Briony, tilting her head back to look up at Rosaleen, "he's *dead*."

Rosaleen's hand swept the air. Briony was lucky to not have to read all the books, but—"She turns him into a bird and he hasn't got any sisters to disenchant him. She has this daughter she wants him to marry, and he won't, so she turns him into a bear. She has a son and decides to poison her stepson, so her son warns his brother, and they run off and marry princesses and never return."

Briony scowled. "All at once?"

"Any *one* would be enough."

Jill, older even than Giles and annoyed he had been the one taken, said, "He should have killed him in a swamp and left his body there. Even if a reed grew up and sang that his son killed him, Prince Henry could denounce it as a lie and execute the shepherd who found it."

Briony's breath puffed out. "King Henry should have sent him for a griffin's feathers. Then he would have been stuck working as a ferryman but he would have lived—"

"Children!" called old Otto. "Move! Your parents will have your heads if you aren't picking the peaches when the church bells chime."

They ran off about her. Rosaleen stood and felt strange.

"And you! Lady Gilliane looked for you when she went to the church!"

Rosaleen sighed. More tales to tell them, after. She grimaced. It wasn't as if she had gone up to the birches, let alone tried to reach the chapel of St. Gualberto. She trudged out of the orchard, down the slope, into the village, down the lanes with hens running across her path, and into the shadow of the church of St. Bernard, where Lady Gilliane talked gravely with a grizzled forester with his cap in hand.

If the tale about fetching the princess as his stepmother were true, Prince Henry—King Henry now—would marry her. Tales of his marriage would be more sure.

As Rosaleen walked up, Lady Gilliane, her hair as white as snow, looked over. "Why, Rosaleen, you look as sad as if some snip of a girl had tricked the prince into forgetting you after you rescued him."

Rosaleen blinked, and said slowly, "Someone's died. Isn't that sad?"

"Somewhat," said Lady Gilliane, "but everyone dies in due course." She nodded to the forester, who nodded to her, sketched a bow to Rosaleen, and headed off. "Especially when you did not even know him, though you met him."

Rosaleen blinked.

"It was hardly a secret, that Giles and his father heard tales about King Henry's death. But you yourself met him before you could possibly remember. Still, it is not much for you to grieve over. Do you even remember Reynold Greenleaf?"

Rosaleen scowled. "Polly's grandfather?"

"He led the men who brought you here. And you saw him sometimes in the next years. But he died, and you do not remember him."

Rosaleen's scowl deepened as she tried to remember.

"Look at the graveyard, and how many graves there are for this little village. There are many, many, many deaths. This one concerns you less than many others." She sighed. "Though what may happen after may be a great concern."

Maid Maleen, thought Rosaleen. But she was not in a tower.

Voices rose as they walked back to the lane. At the end of the town, Giles's father stood, surrounded by anxious adults. They were not talking about some enchanted stepmother, but about armies and what Prince—young King Henry might do with his. Lady Gilliane hurried her on.

As if she could be a proper princess without knowing about kings and queens and princes and princesses. And wars. She had to read about old wars in the library. Why should she not hear about new wars?

Lady Gilliane did not slow.

#

Tales accumulated.

No reed pipe had sung of how King Henry had been murdered. No tales spoke of young King Henry's marvelous beauty, and certainly none of his enchantress bride, or any bride at all.

Some even talked, when they thought she was not listening, about whether he attacked in the borderland, and how the young princes and the king had raised their own soldiers, and whether King Henry intended to send his forces after Princess Rosaleen.

"What good would that do when she slept a hundred years after he captured her?" said a carter, and then it was time for her geography lesson. Up the real hill, on the real road, and into the library. Down to her studies.

Rosaleen sighed as she looked at the maps. Roads, clean and void of dust or mud. Rivers, dry as a bone. Mountains, as flat as pancakes. Forests, as dead as bone.

"It's nicer to learn from the foresters and huntsmen. They take me to rivers and pools." She waved a hand in the air. "It's easier to learn from them."

"You didn't learn to get to the chapel of St. Gualberto from them," said Lady Gilliane. "You learned that from a map."

Rosaleen scowled. She had, but—she might have learned from them—if she had talked often enough—

Lady Gilliane went serenely on. "Water is important. It allows travel more easily than roads. For instance, armies can move by it. Or a princess who is seeking the prince who woke her with a kiss, but was cursed to leave her before she woke up."

Rosaleen looked at the map. That would be much easier if she would know where the prince had to come from. Then she frowned. Her finger went out to touch one waterfall.

Lady Gilliane smiled. "Yes, waterfalls can make it much more difficult. You see the road going about, and how far it must go to make a reasonable path."

"That's the Pine Tree Falls," said Rosaleen.

For a minute, silence reigned.

"It's not so close as the chapel of Saint Gualberto," she said. "But it's close. Even though it's in a different kingdom."

"You can't go on pilgrimage there," said Lady Gilliane.

"I could go on a quest," said Rosaleen.

"To seek your wicked fairy godmother? I do not think she would be impressed that you crossed a kingdom's border. It is not as if the waterfall were thrice ten kingdoms away."

"She promised that I would live happily ever after," said Rosaleen. "Who knows what she might produce to help me?"

"Fairy godmothers," said Lady Gilliane, "show up after the curse that you will sleep is fulfilled."

"If Ella thought that," said Rosaleen, "she would never have gone to the ball."

"She wasn't a princess."

"Some princesses go to balls to win their husbands. There are even—" Rosaleen leaned forward in triumphant memory. "—balls where the bridegroom has been bewitched into forgetting the bride, and is going to marry a false bride, and she has to show up and disenchant him. She could use a fairy godmother's aid."

"But not princesses," said Lady Gilliane. "Stepdaughters of witches, and their daughters, and their maidservants, who learn magic from their mothers or mistresses. Better to avoid that."

She sat back. "And if your heart was truly set on it, you would study the geography to know the way. You already know how to dance."

#

The peach harvest was all but done. Which meant a dance that evening.

Rosaleen skipped down the path toward the village. Already the clouds in the sky turned the color of peaches, and garlands of flowers went up around the square with the bonfire.

To either side, the heaps of wood were being split, vigorously, by young men laughing and urging each other on to greater speed, their axes glinting in the sunset. Young women watched, and giggled, and affixed garlands about the square.

"You fools," snarled an old man, and took a swig from a jug. "What are you doing, gadding about here? Let the king's soldiers come, and they'll march every lad here off to fight the king's war against King Henry."

The young men hesitated in their splitting. One or two began to jeer, that was all talk, they had heard it since King Henry's death.

He waved the jug. "Flee to the mountains, lads! Flee and be free!"

"Better the army than here," said another old man sourly. "Flee to the mountains and you'll come back to find us all dead in our beds, with the houses burned over us. And the harvest stolen, so you starve. Fight in the army, and you can come back and marry your sweethearts."

The old men glared at each other.

"The king's got his army," said a young woman, putting her hands on her hips. "Do you think he pays them to gad about?"

"He'll not send his army here," said a young man. "He'll march us off to fight for him in his castle and let you all die in your bed while we die there."

"Peace." The priest emerged from the church. "Do you quarrel on the saint's doorstep? Must you war here because kings war far away?"

The old men glowered but turned away. The young men turned back to splitting wood, with less talk and fewer smiles. The little children formed circles and sang about bluebirds as they danced, and the older children watched, too old and dignified for that game.

An old shepherd's crook, quite broken, was added to the heap for the bonfire. And two stools that were all but shattered.

Rosaleen skipped up to the children.

An old woman said, "What is she doing here? She should be away by now."

Another one laughed. "Who would know her for the princess?"

The old woman sniffed. "You speak as if she were a bale of cloth, hard to smuggle into a boat and down river. A slip of a girl can be hidden away and should be hidden away."

"That's why she was sent to the mountains," said the other. "To here. To hide her away."

"Safety? If they wanted her in safety, they should have locked her in a tower with a witch to guard her! Young King Henry is already marching with his army!"

"He's not after the princess," said a man of middle years, his black beard vaster than that of any other man Rosaleen had ever seen. She wondered if he were a peddler. He might know more about the kings if he were.

"He might kill her to keep the other prince from claiming her," said grizzled old Rodger. Rosaleen winced.

In the thicket of the crowd, a little girl wailed, and a woman cursed. "You little rascals! Get out of the way! If you—" A woman stood over the children who had danced, and looked about. She pointed at Rosaleen. "Get her to tell you a tale, and stay out of the way."

The old women glanced over and fell silent. Rodger glowered and said, "Don't let them play the tale. They'll get in the way."

The playing children brightened, scrambled over, and begged for a tale, a tale, a tale. The other youngsters followed, as if it were more dignified, and one man dryly said, "Tell them how peaches came to the land."

"Oh, we know *that*," said a boy nearly her age. "A huntsman had a beautiful wife who could turn into a bird, so the king sent him after this strange fruit in hopes he'd die. But his wife told him how to come back with them. And then he sent him after another. And then he sent him after a golden apple."

"A *new* tale!" said a little boy.

"Once upon a time," said Rosaleen, "an old woman had three sons."

"I bet the youngest was simple," grumbled an older boy, folding his arms.

"One day, the king offered a rich reward to anyone who brought him a ship that could sail over land and sea. The oldest son set out at once to the forest, to cut the wood, and met an old man on the way. The old man asked him what he was doing.

"'Going to make rocking horses,' said the oldest, but when he got to the forest, and started to chop, every piece of wood he chopped turned into rocking horses. So he went home in shame—"

"He should have sold the rocking horses!" said a little girl.

"Not everyone is clever enough to see the value of them," said Rosaleen solemnly. "But the middle son thought he would be smarter, and went to the woods, and met the old man who asked him what he was doing.

"'Going to make cuckoo clocks,' said the middle son, but when he got to the forest, and started to chop, every piece of wood he chopped turned into cuckoo clocks. So he went home in shame.

"Then the youngest went, and the older two jeered at him, telling him that the woods were bewitched, but still he went, and met the old man who asked him what he was doing.

"'I'm going to make the king a boat that will sail over land and sea,' said the youngest, and when he got to the forest, and started to chop, every piece of wood he chopped turned into the boat.

"He sailed it over land and sea to the king, who gave him a rich reward, and he bought a fine farm and married a good bride and lived happily ever after."

"He should go looking for enchanted spectacles," said Giles. "Those are different and would let him see everything in the world."

"That," said Rosaleen, severely, "would depend on what the enchantment was." She hesitated and then remembered a tale. "The spectacles can't see a pin that hid in a princess's hair, for one, if she's using the spectacles."

She would not have done as that princess did, she told herself virtuously. Even if she had owned the magical book. Telling men they had to find her three times, and then they had to hide themselves so she could not find them three times, or she would cut their heads off.

She would not want to marry a prince who would want to marry a princess who would cut her suitors' heads off.

"He was a simpleton to just tell what he was doing," said one boy, loftily.

"He was *clever*," said another. "He heard his brothers' tales, he knew what to do to succeed."

"That's not clever," said Giles. "I heard of a *clever* hero in the town."

Rosaleen blinked in surprise.

"Once upon a time, a widow had three sons. They set out to seek their fortunes so as to not burden their mother, and the two older ones took big bundles of food that their mother gave them, and the youngest told their mother that he could get his own food and would not burden her by taking hers.

"So at the crossroads, the older brothers said they all had to take different ways, and they sent the younger brother up into the wild hills. Where there were giants.

"He stayed in a cave, where he found there were rooms full of copper, and of silver, and of gold. The giants caught him, and told him he could stay with them as long as he worked, he would be their watchman. They gave him a table and told him to rap on it and say, 'The meal of a king!' whenever he wanted to eat.

"For many a day, he served them like this, doing nothing much, but after a time, he decided it was too dull, living there. So he took the table as his wages and set out to return home. On the way he met a hermit living in the mountain, and he took out his table, and they ate a royal feast that it made.

"The hermit had a horn, that whenever he blew it, summoned up an army, and he offered the youngest son it in return for the table. The youngest son took it, but when he had gone a day from the hermit's cave, he blew the horn. A company of soldiers in shining armor appeared, and he ordered them to take the table back.

"So he returned home and lived well. Soldiers of the king were nearby, and they told the king that there was this peasant boy who ate the dinners of a king, and no one knew how. The king sent word that he wished to see the marvel.

"He sent the table, but told the king that if he did not return it, he would make war on him. The king thought that was ludicrous, and made a table exactly like the first to send back, but the boy realized, as soon as it was returned, that it was not the magical table he had sent." He spread his arms. "The boy blew on the horn until he had a vast army, and marched on the king. Who was so terrified that he offered the boy half of his kingdom and his daughter's hand in marriage, and the whole of the kingdom after his death."

Much exclamation followed.

Giles looked at Rosaleen. "You might marry a boy like that."

Rosaleen shrugged. She had heard that tale. "His wife wormed out of him how he had gotten the table and the horn, and was shocked that he had stolen them and attacked her father for stealing. He sent word to the hermit, who came to the city and ate every day at the table. And he sent word to the giants, who sent back word that the table only made food for humans, not for giants, and because he left their gold and their silver and their copper, they didn't mind."

The children exclaimed again about how sensible the giants were, and whether it was true that giants didn't eat the same food as men. Giles looked sour.

And, Rosaleen thought, people were done decking the square.

Polly called, "Oh, look!"

The small children scrambled off to dance again, and she joined the older boys and girls who were far too old to play a game of Sally Go Round the Sun. The younger ones were soon tumbling to the ground in it and laughing. It had not taken them too long to get to a speed where they tripped. The maidens had all vanished, she slowly realized, and then laughter resounded.

Rosaleen blinked. The maidens poured into the square, and all showed off their gowns and hair, adorned with ribbons in every brilliant shade, woven in elaborate patterns.

She was too young for something so fancy. And the ladies would sniff and say that the princess should not wear something so common.

A fiddler began to play, and the larger figures started to form. Rosaleen went to join the first, stately dances, such that even the oldest villagers would dance, and only the very youngest sit out.

"Ho, what's going on at the castle?" said one man. He looked up, shifting through the forming measures in a way that broke them up, and all sorts of gazes followed him. Rosaleen frowned. The people at the castle milled around like people who heard news. Some—even at this distance, she could see how one of them started to wring her hands and turned away from the people talking. Rosaleen flinched. Who heard bad news.

Someone broke off from the crowd—a young man—and started up the way. The dance did not begin again. Low voices started about Rosaleen, as people glanced at children and pulled back before talking of how the valley was not hidden, it was just in the mountains.

The young man came running down. "The king is summoning the gentlemen to serve in his army! King Henry is coming to attack!"

Some village women started to weep and wring their hands, and throw themselves at young men. An older woman talked about how the king would not summon peasants from hither and yon when he had knights to deal with the problem, and other old women looked disapproving. Rosaleen bit her lip. King Henry could raise peasants, and her father would need to, to face his numbers.

One little boy said fiercely, "If I were king, I would not let anything stand in my way of stopping the wicked king!"

\#

It was odd, thought the Fairy of Pine Tree Falls. The girl trudging up the mountain road did not look out of the ordinary. Her progress was, nevertheless, what the pool choose to show her.

The fairy made one more try to shake the vision, to look at anything else on the mountain, but nothing came. So she settled and watched. Seeing important things was its greatest virtue.

She studied the girl and the road about her. The mist was thick enough that even a woodsman would need to take care, but the girl did well enough. Not perhaps quite so well as a woodsman.

A woodsman's daughter whose father had made a bargain with a bear that he could marry her? But she was too young. The fairy sat back, letting the picture fade away. Thus, she knew that the girl had yet to chase after her bridegroom who had been turned into a bear, and whose curse *would* have broken if only she had waited another fortnight.

She gazed at the ferns ahead. Perhaps her mother had stolen from a witch's garden. Perhaps the mother had, instead of telling her daughter to tell the witch to take her due, actually told her daughter about promising her to the witch in return for being spared, and the girl had run away. The girl was, if anything, a little old for that.

The fairy stood. It was not worth it, trying to induce the pool to show the girl more clearly. The clearest image would not show what she wished to know. Far, far, far better to go and see her.

"Meeting them on the way is better than becoming their godmothers, anyway," she muttered. And seeing them without being seen was wiser than meeting them unawares.

Reaching the misty forest and standing, hidden, among the trees was a matter of moments, and then she could critically watch as the girl walked onward.

She might have convinced herself that the girl was a shepherdess seeking out a lamb if the girl had looked around, trying to peer through the mists and the trees, but the girl trudged steadily onward and searched for nothing but the way. She had dressed warmly enough for the weather, too.

How intriguing. Other fairies might have watched and not cared, but she thought she needed to know what this girl meant to do. And why.

The fairy slipped among the trees. The best place was probably among the boulders, where she could see the crossroads, and the trees' shadows helped hide her from sight.

The girl reached the crossroads—the fairy wondered if she had seen her before—and with only a glance at signpost, she picked her way. Then her eyes narrowed as she looked about on the road with more care than at the sign. The fairy drifted closer as the girl began to mutter to herself. It was the matter of a moment to give herself a guise that she could let the girl see.

"No castle. Then, they often don't. They can live in little cottages so you do not respect them, and then you're in trouble."

Then the girl saw her, and blinked. "I beg your pardon, granny." The words sounded stilted. "I did not intend to be so rude. I am deeply troubled at heart."

There were a number of tales that the child could have been quoting. Many a prudent prince, or princess, had said them before.

The fairy contented herself with saying, "You seem unfamiliar with this land."

"Oh, yes," said the girl. "I have read the maps, but I have not been here before. It is not the same. It never is." She looked up at the towering trees. "I might be safer here. With King Henry and his armies everywhere." She eyed the waterfall, vaguely visible among the trees. "I suppose I was lucky to not have a storm come and—" She waved her hands. "Fill up the river, knock down the trees, strike me with lightning. I didn't see any shelter."

This one did not seem to be on any quest. "Perhaps, then, you should go back."

The girl scowled. "That wouldn't be right. A princess has to care about her kingdom. The princes are too busy fighting King Henry. The king too. They won't go off on quests."

"Usually princesses look for their husbands, as princes look for their brides," said the fairy, dryly. *And are older than you are*, she thought. *But a princess of this age—*

"I'm looking for a bugle," said the girl. Rosaleen, the fairy realized with a jolt. It had to be. "One that summons an army when blown."

The fairy raised an eyebrow. *Not a modest request.*

Rosaleen sighed and looked about at the trees again. "And this is not my kingdom, and I don't know much about it, and I'm safer here. Like Maid Maleen out of her tower."

She sighed again and sat down on a stone. "Maybe I should go on and get a job as a scullery maid. Then I could fall asleep somewhere where the prince could wake me up and then I could win him by going to a ball. At least I know that the other servants wouldn't slander me to the queen mother about how much I could spin and weave and sew."

She looked back down into the valley, through the gap the road opened. "But I probably shouldn't. I need the bugle to defend the castle. The king and the princes won't. They're too busy down in the valleys, and it's not a valuable castle, or they wouldn't have sent me there. But I should try to defend it, and the bugle is the only way I can think of."

Had the girl even needed to breathe during that? thought the fairy.

"And then I have to go find the prince after. I would need an army for that, it's not safe."

"It's not like princesses don't fare far on their own," said the fairy.

"It's dangerous. They could meet a witch who traps them. That prince would have to rescue me twice. And that wasn't part of the curse. That's for princesses who fumble breaking a curse on a bear or a lion or—something. It's not me, and I shouldn't count on it."

She sighed. "Happy ever after," she said gloomily. "But sometimes the prince dies or something and I don't want that first."

"When you've been cursed to sleep? My child, have you ever heard of a princess who had to deal with a witch after that?"

Rosaleen said, with new brightness, "There was a prince who had to deal with a witch in the forest and then met with a princess who was a swan and with her help managed to defeat her father and rescue her so nothing came of meeting the witch. I think that happens more often than they tell, they just leave it out of the story, because it sounds stupid. The other children wouldn't play it because they thought it was stupid."

The fairy raised an eyebrow. Rosaleen had learned more in this mountain refuge than she would have in her father's castle. Still, she might not be the wisest person to use the horn.

"So you will drive off King Henry's forces before you sleep?"

"Then someone could steal it while I slept. Giants probably." Rosaleen threw her hands in the air. "And maybe some cowherd or gardener's boy would steal it back from the giants but I need it to find my prince since it's going to be a prince that I marry and not a cowherd or gardener's boy. However noble and valiant."

Then she eyed the fairy sideways. As if, despite all her studies, it were just occurring to her why it was so crucial to always be courteous to an old woman she met on the way.

"Your great-grandfather had such a horn," said the fairy, gravely. Rosaleen, tilting her head to one side, listened with silent attention. "But he put it away so securely that your father could not find it."

Rosaleen groaned. "I should run away. Find dwarfs who live in the woods. Or bandits, but I don't know how to win them over. Forest knights, then. Or even dragons. I could hide out with any of them, and sleep there, but I can't find them. At least my parents didn't send me out to find strawberries in the snow, and gave me a dress of paper to do it in. I'd find dwarfs then, but they'd only help me with strawberries, and then I'd go back."

"There are no such dwarfs in this forest," said the fairy. "You would freeze."

Rosaleen sighed. "And I would have to be polite anyway. I talk too much, I would not win them over."

The fairy smiled. "At least you do not keep secrets."

"I couldn't steal it from bandits, or go to I Know Not Where and Bring Back I Know Not What. And no one is giving it to me."

"Oh, no one would give you such a thing."

Rosaleen looked desolate.

"Instead, you will get three."

Rosaleen blinked. She did not crow, but she looked with dawning hope.

"Here is a horn," said the fairy. "If you blow it once, it will summon a soldier. Twice, a company. Thrice, a troop. Four times a regiment. Five times, an army."

Rosaleen reached out slowly, as if she feared that the horn would put forth wings and fly away, but her fingers closed on it slowly. It came, of course, with a strap which she put over her shoulder.

"And here are two plants. This rose bush you must plant outside the castle. And this sapling you must plant in its garden."

"Oh, how can I carry them? I could rip my skirt to make a bag for them, but they might fall out."

"And here is a bag. That is not a gift. I will reclaim it when you are done." She smiled. "If you act with all due haste, not before."

#

Rosaleen carefully took the bag. Her heart hammered in her chest. It had hammered all the time she had prattled. She kept her head bent to hide her face, because she had to be blushing. To prattle like that—like a baby, or a girl too proud of her lessons—

She knelt. It hid her face and let her carefully put both plants in the bag so that she could carry them both upright. Then she stood and carefully hefted the bag. She could carry it.

The fairy still smiled benignly on her, and still looked like an old woman. Rosaleen forced her breath out. Perhaps she should still not admit that the disguise was thin.

"I thank you. My own godmother could not have taken better care of me than you with these gifts."

#

The sky turned as brilliantly colorful as a queen's wardrobe, showing how late she was. Rosaleen bit her lip and trudged on. This hill looked familiar—and then she looked down the slope in relief. The castle in sight, just past the village—the sunset was still bright enough to show that clearly. She would be glad of supper and bed. She started to trudge down.

Then a shout resounded, and people scrambled from their homes. Other children reached her first, exclaiming over her, some touching her arm to be certain that it was her. One girl started to cry, and Polly and Briony exclaimed over how wonderful it was that she was safe and sound.

Then the adults followed.

She had to fight to keep the bag and its precious plants safe from the press of the crowd. For a moment, she wished she had put it somewhere safe before they saw her, but then plants might be no safer than brides, left alone in a strange place. She clutched the bag again and shouted.

"It's a gift from a fairy! I must keep it safe!"

When large hands came about her waist from behind, she started. When the blacksmith lifted her to his shoulder and forged into the crowd, she breathed a sigh of relief. Servants from the castle thronged with the villagers, and there were a few faces she did not recognize. Peddlers? New servants? They were oddly short. It was hard to think in this din, as they all cheered and shouted about her. A maid from the castle scurried up the slope toward it, calling something about the princess.

The ladies appeared by the doorway, but only Lady Gilliane came down.

"Your Highness! What happened with you?"

"Fairies!" said Rosaleen. "I have to plant plants!"

The crowd grew quiet, gawking at her. Had even the blacksmith heard her when she said it earlier?

She hooked the bag's strap and held it up. Leaves showed. Murmurs spread about the crowd. Someone said something about gardeners.

Lady Gilliane said, "Let me hear your tale. Unless it is so urgent that we will all turn invisible, and you into an ugly beast, if I do."

#

At the table, the sunset could be seen through the window. Lady Gilliane's attention was wholly on her. It felt harder to tell the story than to talk to the fairy feigning to be an old woman. Still the sunshine had not completely vanished by the time she finished her tale.

"So it won't do to be lazy," said Rosaleen. "We must plant these at once." She scowled at the open bag on the table. The plants looked flourishing, not suffering at all from being lugged down the mountain-side in a bag. Maybe it was unwise to bring them into the library, but she and Lady Gilliane could talk secretly nowhere else.

Lady Gilliane sighed.

"Perhaps that means in the morning," said Rosaleen. "Because it would be very silly to plant them wrong. After all that."

"Very silly indeed," said Lady Gilliane, dryly. She touched a leaf of the sapling.

"That must be an apple tree, from the leaves," said Rosaleen, "but it still has to be planted in the garden, not an orchard."

"Very true," said Lady Gilliane and sat back. "What will you do with the horn?"

"Hide it," said Rosaleen, promptly. "It was important to find it, but that's so I have it when I need it. A princess should not be so easy to startle as a rabbit."

"Which tale did you read that in?"

"I forget which. But an army might draw an army."

Lady Gilliane raised an eyebrow. "You are in great fortune. While you were gone, seven new servants arrived. Four men and three women. All rather short, but the men are sturdy gardeners nonetheless. There will be no difficulty in digging the holes. Even by lantern light."

"Then," said Rosaleen, "I don't even need to rest." She hopped up. So those were the small figures she had seen.

Lady Gilliane did not stand. "The fairy told you that the horn would summon soldiers. Did she tell you how to send them back?"

Rosaleen's heart seemed to stop before hammering. No, she had not. A mill grinding out salt could turn the sea salt. An army who came from nowhere and did not go back. . . .

"But *why*? They always go back in the tales."

"Perhaps it's a test."

Rosaleen scowled. What a perfectly awful test. "I'm going to read the books again. They wouldn't hide such things. If the soldiers can go away again, they will talk about it."

"Sometimes," said Lady Gilliane, "burning the frog's skin saves the bride to be a woman forever. Sometimes it kills her. You should know better."

Rosaleen felt her face setting in grumpy lines. And she couldn't blow the horn too late, either, even if she had to do something with the soldiers after.

"For now, at the least, you have to talk to the gardeners first. Whether to plant in the open, or in a recess, or where the earth is damp, or sheltered from wind."

"She didn't tell me anything," said Rosaleen. "More than outside the castle and in the garden."

"Rest assured, the gardeners will tell you everything that she did not." Lady Gilliane sighed. "Probably three times over. They have quite definite opinions. It does no good to tell them that we have quite adequate apples from the orchard, or that we do not need better onions. They are digging, weeding, pruning, mulching."

Rosaleen thought for a moment. "My mother sent them?"

"Of course," said Lady Gilliane. "Listen." She waved at the window.

A cheery song rose outside. Rosaleen looked. Four men, the tallest of whom could barely reach the height of her elbow, all them wearing green, were gathered about dug-up earth in the vegetable garden. Creating a new bed, she thought. She also thought they were done for the day.

"I'll have to tell them the fairy said it needed to be done quickly."

Lady Gilliane raised an eyebrow.

"And ask whether the morning will be soon enough."

"They will no doubt regale you with any number of tales," added Lady Gilliane. "They are quite keen on gardening. And—dear child—now that you have been given what you need by a fairy, there is no need for you to gallivant all over the land without so much as telling anyone that you were leaving."

Rosaleen flushed a little as she picked up the bag. She had told Lady Gilliane that she needed to visit the falls, she thought resentfully.

The short men turned from the garden as she came out. They were all knotted with muscle, and had hair and beards of brown—one light brown, one almost black, and the other two just brown— and their weathered faces were an interesting sort of ugly as they turned them solemnly toward her.

Rosaleen, holding the bag, said, "These are the plants I received from the Fairy of the Pine Falls. I need to plant them, the tree in the garden and rose outside the walls." She bit her lip, looking for strange face to face. "The fairy said that they needed to be planted quickly, but the morning might suffice."

"An apple tree that is," said one. "You're closest, Rob, be sure of it." They talked in low voices, of places and reasons, of sunlight and water, and she followed little of it. At least she heard the names. Rob, and Adam, and Ned, and Tom. Though she was not sure she could lay a name to any of their faces.

In a lull, she said, "She's also going to reclaim the bag."

"Unwise to ignore her injunctions," said one solemnly.

Rob, she thought after a minute, one of the two with just brown hair. Ned, with the pale brown hair, was the one saying that the light was fading fast, and no one would prescribe that quickly for planting—she thought.

"They survived a long journey. Careful placing'll keep them through the night."

"Pshaw," said dark-haired Tom. "No one should give the princess a poor impression of our skills. We could plant these by lamplight if the moon were new."

"Ah," said Adam, "but surely the princess will want to oversee the planting? She was the one who had the plants put into her hands, and heard the directions. She will not want to slough off the task, even if she accepts that we are better at the digging. *And*—she walked all day. And hasn't eaten yet."

"And who," said Rob, "gets to tell Ellen she hasn't eaten, and isn't going to eat?'

The short men nodded solemnly and escorted her toward the kitchen even as they discussed where the best places were.

"South side," said Ned. "For the rose."

"In the sun," said Adam, nodding.

"And shielded from the north wind," said Rob. He waved a hand toward the north. "South side is mostly safe, but we need to be sure."

"The tree will be easier," said Tom, "because it goes in the garden with shelter to all sides."

"It will still need the sun," said Ned, scowling. He looked about at the flower beds growing indistinct in the dark. "And it needs to not shade the flowers, either. Unless we have to. It's more important than the flowers, but there's no need to sacrifice them unless we have to. We do have to put them both in the sun."

Adam rolled his eyes and turned to Rosaleen. "Here's where we will leave the plants for the night." He reached out his arms, and Rosaleen gave him the bag, which he hefted with an ease that she envied.

Ned started to discuss where the rose might go in particular, and they were instantly raising objections and points and wrangling like generals about armies.

Laughter came from the kitchens. A woman even shorter than the men, and somewhat less muscular, and blond of hair, looked out and shook her head, but her voice was filled with mirth.

"Your Highness! Have a peach tart. They will debate for hours, and the Fairy herself could not stop them."

Rosaleen walked over. The tart was still warm from the oven, and two other women were hard at work among bowls and spoons. One of them was as brown-haired as Adam and Rob, but one had red hair.

"I do hope you like tarts," said the blond one, who had addressed her.

"They said you did," said the red-haired woman, glowering, "but you know how untrustworthy they can be."

Rosaleen assured them that she did.

The blond one, though her apron was spotted with flour, did not turn back to the kitchen. She wiped her hands off, sighed with contentment, and glanced sideways at Rosaleen.

"Going to want pies from the tree?"

Rosaleen hesitated, ransacking her thoughts. She had been filled with thoughts of the horn and the danger and that the woman was a fairy. She hadn't been thinking of fruits and pies.

The red-haired woman, without looking up from her bowl, said, "You should introduce yourself, first, Molly." She glanced over her shoulder. "I'm Ellen."

"And I am Amy," said the third, chopping still. "But we will need to know whether the apples are too magical to touch."

After a minute, Rosaleen said, "She didn't say I couldn't use the apples."

"Ah, yes, she." Molly laughed a little. "I suppose they will treat the apple as something won from a monster if we try to offer it up at the table."

"She didn't say it would have apples, either," said Rosaleen. "She didn't even say it was an apple tree. I guessed that from the leaves."

"A prudent princess, to have noticed with such care," said Amy. "It's likely to bear apples in its own time, though. All apple trees do."

"Can't they produce other things?" said Rosaleen. "Like golden apples?"

"Still apples," said Ellen.

"Or diamonds—or candles—"

"Then it's not an apple tree," said Ellen.

"Could look like one until it fruits," said Amy, thoughtfully.

"Such is the plague of plants," said Molly expansively. "Some things can be told from a mere sprout, and some wait until the very end. Come, Your Highness, tell me whether the tart is good. I'm not certain of this batch."

Rosaleen nibbled. A log in the fire snapped, and a plume of brilliant orange sparks went up the chimney.

Molly said, judiciously, "If your brothers want to be brave knights, they will have to set on bolder quests than yours."

Rosaleen looked at her hands. "They're young yet."

"You're young."

"They're younger than me." She nibbled on the tart. It was hard to care about brothers she had never met. "I suppose they've told them all sorts of tales about how a princess was locked in a tower because fairies told her parents that she would be a peril to her brothers, but the parents didn't tell her brothers. So as soon as the king and queen died, the brothers let her out, and then the princess knew nothing and—" She waved her hand. "—was a peril to them both."

"Foolish," said Ellen. "Never any point trying to avert those things."

"They asked," said Rosaleen. "The king and queen. The fairies tried to not tell them, but they insisted on learning." She licked her fingers. "They should have told the princes. If they were going to be so silly as to lock her up."

Then she sighed. Her parents had told her brothers, she knew. And her brothers would not be so fond of her that they would let her out of the mountains. And it might not matter if they did. Perhaps they would decide to let her out only for the messenger to fall asleep while arriving. It was the sort of thing that fairy spells did.

She looked back to where Adam had put the bag with the two plants. Then she blinked. The plants were there, but the bag was gone. That had been—quick.

#

It was warm enough that she could gambol on the grass without her shoes, however much the other ladies grumbled that a princess should always go shod. Especially at her age, when she should care whether she looked childish.

She frolicked out, childishly, to the rose bushes, in full bloom. The petals were pink and peach, shading from one to the other, and nodding in every breeze. One branch was a vivid scarlet, and the gardeners nodded solemnly and talked of how such things happened.

"Come look at this, Rosaleen!" called Briony. Rosaleen ran to see how the vines had draped over a scowling little troll statue, now looking enraged at the flowers, and they laughed and laughed.

"Come, Rosaleen," said Lady Gilliane, from a window where the branches were encroaching. "Didn't you learn your lessons? Don't you know that your prince must find you? How can he if the castle is wrapped in roses?"

"Oh, there must be a way," said Rosaleen, twirling about. Her hair caught on a rose, and she freed it. "The fairy said so. And there must be a way for him to get out too, or he won't be able to get far away. It's my getting out that after might be a problem." She pondered. "I shall put pruning hooks in my room, where I can find them again."

"As long as the gardeners don't find them first," said Polly. "They need to prune plants."

"I shall get new ones," said Rosaleen. "I can afford that. And I have time enough, I think." She put her finger to her mouth. "I know. I shall ask the gardeners which would be the best pruning hooks. Then they will put them in the room themselves, and go to get more."

Adam's voice floated over the roses. "A crafty plan, Your Highness."

#

Snow blew by the window, where roses were dried and dead in a frame about it. Rosaleen could see the sky, leaden gray and featureless. The gray daylight had not changed over the hours. She could not measure the passing of time by it.

In the bed, Lady Gilliane coughed, feebly.

Rosaleen let the curtain drop over the window and came back to the bed. Maids stopped fussing over the bed curtains, and Rosaleen swallowed. Lady Gilliane looked only a little less pale than the sheets. The priest had come and gone.

Her eyes were alert, though.

"I—" She coughed a little. "I have a gift for you, Rosaleen."

Rosaleen tilted her head to one side. An odd time to give it. She could have—Rosaleen's mouth tightened—made it a bequest.

"Take this handkerchief," said Lady Gilliane.

Rosaleen obeyed. Plain, white, nicely hemmed, but without so much as a monogram. It could not be meant as a memento, she thought, and felt chilled. She looked up.

"It's magic." Lady Gilliane coughed again. "Take this handkerchief, throw it on the floor, and ask a question. Whoever answers you falsely and walks over the handkerchief will fall down and break his leg."

Rosaleen looked at it for a minute. "Is there some kind of trick? Why I have never seen you use it?"

Lady Gilliane managed a weak smile. "The trick of it is—you can only ask one question, ever. Though you can ask that question as many times as you wish, of as many as you wish." She let her head fall back on the pillow. "It was a fairy gift. Three generations ago."

In that time, no one had wanted a question answered so badly as to risk never being able to use it again. As for her, she knew her tales.

"'Are you the prince who visited my castle?'"

Lady Gilliane laughed, faintly, and her eyes closed.

A few hours later, a lady in waiting bustled Rosaleen off to bed, arguing that she needed her sleep. Rosaleen lay abed long enough to see the servants off, and then slipped up to put the handkerchief carefully with the horn, in the satchel.

For a moment, she stood in the middle of the room. A lady in waiting would send her back to bed if she left, and she thought sadly, she could do nothing.

In the morning, a maid thought to tell her that Lady Gilliane had died.

#

With the thaws of spring came the rumors from the valleys. Tales of armies and fighting and ruin. Rosaleen felt glad that the mountain castle was cut off by rivers and narrow roads as well as distance.

The murmurs among the servants spoke less of gratitude and more of fear.

Snow melted more quickly than usual, putting the rivers and streams in full spate. They flooded far more than the common spots. The villagers even talked of how bridges might wash out.

"Don't make deals with the Devil to mend them," said Rosaleen pertly, and got some laughter.

When rumor spoke of a muddy route out, a boy vanished from among the servants. Some remembered that he had talked of a cousin.

So, thought Rosaleen, my mother was wrong when she thought orphans were free of attachments. She wondered who else would flee.

Long before the summer, the disappearances grew into a flood. Some asked for leave, but she thought they would have gone even if refused it. The villagers, at least, stayed, and so, oddly enough, did the last seven servants who arrived.

Who were, Rosaleen remembered, akin to each other.

It felt odd to walk about the castle without a single lady in waiting, little though they had done when they were here. One day, she slipped down a corridor and into the garden. Ned crawled under bushes, claiming something about weeds and how there was not enough diligence about them. Tom said that he would check the other bushes at once. Rob smiled and tipped his cap to her before returning to weeding a flower bed. The smell of dinner wafted out of the kitchen. Then she blinked and hurried forward.

The tree did indeed have buds on it, among its leaves. Small, red as roses, but it would have flowers. Perhaps fruit.

She giggled. Perhaps candles.

She walked away, realized she drifted toward the kitchen, where the cooks all stirred some dishes, and said, "When will dinner be ready?"

"In an hour, Your Highness!" called Molly. "It's easy with so few."

Rosaleen bit her lip in realization. "Don't you want to leave?"

Silence fell.

"You do know what the curse will do to anyone here?" said Rosaleen.

"We have no family but each other," called Rob.

Ned, his shovel half-driven into the earth, put his foot on it and turned the earth. "And where would we go with King Henry making as much trouble as he does? It's not like nobles take on many gardeners, least of all strangers who come like beggars. Or cooks, either."

Amy called, "Should we heat water for your bath after dinner? It will be easy enough today."

Rosaleen looked among them. She could not force them to leave. And they had never lied to her. She turned back to the cook and said, "Yes, I would be grateful."

#

The garden held hundreds of autumnal flowers, but not enough to keep it as brilliant as the summer. Green leaves, from plants where the flowers gone to seed, filled many flower beds. Rosaleen sat, mending her gown, in the window seat, and her gaze slipped by both flowers and greenery, to the tree.

Geese honked overhead, the skein a mere suggestion against the clouds. Winter was coming, and the tree's apples had ripened, and turned golden.

They often vanished. Rosaleen felt quite certain that they had not been made into pies.

"Dinner!" called Molly from the doorway, and Rosaleen laid aside the sewing with relief. After, she would go for a walk and sew no more today.

A plate and cup of pewter. Not wood, not gold and crystal. As usual.

"I should run away and become a scullery maid," she said. She did housework now, there were so few servants.

"Unwise now," said Amy. "How would you find another castle before the snow hit?"

Hurry, thought Rosaleen, but did not say. It might be possible to escape the mountains before snowfall, but it would be silly to try without good reason. She took another bite. All the more after all she had done to get those roses, and that tree.

She looked over. Something glinted in the tree.

On its own, not with the sunlight glinting off the leaves or the apples. A firebird, bright as a burning coal, eyed her before hiding among the leaves.

Rosaleen rolled her eyes. "I suppose a firebird stealing the apples is only fitting for a tree given you by a fairy."

"At least it's not a mermaid trying to seduce your prince away," said Amy.

"Or a dragon wanting a maiden to be offered to him," said Rosaleen. She ate. Then she yawned.

"I think I will rest this afternoon. I hope I'm not falling ill."

Molly murmured agreement, casting a sidelong glance at her as she swept off with the dishes. Rosaleen grimaced. She hoped the seven didn't fall ill. The villagers might help, but they were not her servants.

In her chamber, her gaze went out to the window. The firebird lofted its wings, and flew. In the shadows, it gleamed all over, brightly, and when it flew into the sun, the radiance was bright enough to be seen against the sunlight. Rosaleen yawned again. Her bed was over there. She stumbled over, just barely slipping off her shoes before she slid onto the bed.

Part III

Sunlight slanted over the kitchen from the windows. Roses already grew over them. Not a single cook was cooking, or taking out food to cook. The gardeners gathered about the door.

"Did you feel it?" said Rob—the Dwarf of Pine Mountain. His gaze went over the kitchen. He wondered if they would be there, inside the bounds of the spells, were it not for the danger of villagers seeing them and wondering why the enchantment did not catch them. Explaining would be out of the question. They might tell Rosaleen.

Ellen, the Dwarf of Iris Pond, put down the dishes she had cleaned. "I saw it. She was yawning away."

"Then there's nothing for it but to put the clean dishes away and be done," said Molly, the Dwarf of the Mountain Birches. She pushed off the counter she leaned on.

"We haven't eaten dinner ourselves," said Amy, the Dwarf of Moon Lake, but she did not reach for a pot.

"The fairy of Pine Trees Falls," said the Dwarf of Mountain Birches, "said we should come and eat with her." Molly. How easy it had been to fall into the human names, and how easy it was keep falling back.

From the doorway, Ned, Dwarf of Diamond Mines, looked at her, and his eyebrows went up. "Without considering the roses?"

"She planned them," said Tom, the Dwarf of Gray River, "and we did nothing to them while planting them. That should suffice."

"At that," said Adam, the Dwarf of Apple Orchard Hill, "we will eat dinner with her. She can tell us what needs to be done. If anything."

Rob snorted. "And perhaps beg us for help."

"You know as well as she does," said the Dwarf of Apple Orchard Hill, "that the conquest of this kingdom would not go well for us. Least of all if King Henry manages to claim Princess Rosaleen as a bride."

"But coming and going," said the Dwarf of Moon Pool, "will not be so difficult for us as it was her." Amy's hand swept toward where Rosaleen slept. "And she managed it in no more than a day."

Rob wondered if he would think of them by their human names forever. Then he snorted. Or even whether he, himself, would forget that he had been Rob instead of the Dwarf of Pine Mountain, though he had been the Dwarf of Pine Mountain for centuries, and might be for millennia yet.

"We shall have to keep watch," said Ned. "True, the gap between the prince's arrival and when she wakens will aid us, but watch is necessary."

"Perhaps the fairy will aid us," said Adam.

"Perhaps not," said Ellen. "Let us go to receive her hospitality."

#

The air felt damp, but the cave was deep enough that the torrents of water did not splatter them. Or perhaps the fairy used magic. Certainly the cave was lit brightly by the sunlight that lit up the falls as fiery white, set with rainbows.

Among its other comforts.

She must have watched the pool, thought the Dwarf of the Moon Pool. The table bore a joint of beef lay with gravy beside it, and bread and apple butter, and a salad, and jugs of cider, all ready. Then she rolled her eyes. The fairy must have felt the curse gathering, to have fixed this all in time. She and the others had felt it months ago, to take up their positions.

Unwise to ponder their fortune while the others ate. She dug in before they emptied every dish and vessel. Still, every now and again, she glanced about. She had seen them more these last months than ever before. She had called them more by their assumed names than by their own.

She bit into a slice of bread with apple butter. Perhaps she would never stop thinking of them by those names. Perhaps even she would continue to think of herself as Amy.

It would do her no harm. She ate.

Finally, the Dwarf of Diamond Mines, Ned, pushed back his plate. "A good meal, a good meal—but not a wise arrangement. The princess will know that something is up when she wakes up and we're not there, waking up, but instead show up without waking up."

Then, it would be wiser to think of them by their human names. She was Amy, and he was Ned, and she did not want to slip up before Rosaleen. Perhaps the princess guessed, but she should learn the truth at the end, if at all.

Adam shrugged. "She saw the firebird fly off. Tell her we were lucky to escape the same way."

"It's magical," said Tom. He grinned.

"We're not," said Ellen. "Unless you want to tell her that."

Even Molly shook her head, and Tom sank down a little.

"The firebird could feel the spell," added Ellen, "but she had no reason to think we can—or that we can ignore it safely, as the firebird could not."

"Dumb luck would do it," said Tom.

Amy frowned. "She may not notice. She's no fool, but she doesn't study things to ferret out secrets like that. Like winter's snow in the heat of midsummer, her notions will melt away if we do not give her reason to ponder them deeply."

"We've all been outside before," said Molly. "Considering meals. The thing is, if we keep close enough watch, we just have to rub our eyes as we walk in on her."

"And yawn," said Tom.

"It will at least raise doubt," said Ned.

This brought general agreement, but at the end, Rob sighed. "The worst of it is, that it's not even helping with the war. The kingdoms are not better off."

"What could have be done about King Henry?" Molly waved her hand and the bread and butter in it. "Either of them? Too late to be a fairy godmother, even if they would believe us."

"At least," said the Fairy of the Pine Tree Falls, judiciously, "we are not making matters of politics and war any worse."

"They are decided about where the prince is to come from," said Ned. "The Fairy of Cherry Blossom Hill works the hardest, but they are tying up every prince for as far as they can reach. By tying the knot."

Molly rolled her eyes. "You never saw so many balls."

"As if that were a problem!" said Amy. "They are ensuring a fine crop of princes. A choice array." She waved her hand at the fairy. "She prudently put no time in the curse. Rosaleen can sleep a hundred years and a day, for one of their great-great-grandsons."

The Fairy of Pine Tree Falls smiled a little and nodded in gracious acknowledgment.

"If it comes to that," said Adam, "perhaps she could be rescued by a woodcutter's son, or a soldier who left the army?" He cocked an eyebrow.

"No," said the Fairy of Pine Tree Falls. "I did specify a prince."

"And," said Rob, his mug of cider in hand, "a prince will have a kingdom. Which will help protect her from—" He waved. "—King Henry. If it takes long enough that the king's not a danger, there's plenty of room for princes." He drank.

"Why waste time?" said the Fairy of Pine Tree Falls. "I have some leeway, but why would I allow King Henry to do his worst? Like a fool standing about gawking without realizing that the ogre eating his companion can eat him next? He will have a strong army after."

"Not if the fighting goes on this way," said Ellen.

"Unwise to risk it," said the fairy, firmly. "Some things can hasten the day. Several things, in fact."

#

At the cottage in the woods, there were owls in the trees, robins on the garden fence, sparrows flitting through the air, and doves on the roof.

"This does not appear in most tales," said the old man, leaning on his staff in the midst of his vegetable garden.

"This gets omitted," said the fairy, "because they never hear of it. Any prince who blunders on you tells how you live in this cottage—" She waved her hand at it. "—and can summon all the birds of the air—" She waved her hand at them. "—to tell him things. If he even asks about me, he probably won't repeat it." She scowled. "I suppose a princess would do the same, but they generally don't blunder on you."

He chuckled. "So my sisters tell me."

A raven cawed in vigorous agreement.

"From your sister?"

"Nah, just likes to caw. He's not even telling me where to send the prince."

"Just as well. I am looking for a prince to send."

The man raised an eyebrow. "By all accounts, neither your gift nor her curse carried a time limit."

"I wish to hasten the hour. With the way the other fairies are moving, the prince will certainly need the advice of the man who can speak to all the birds in the world, and his brothers who can speak to all the beasts in the world, and all the fish in the world, because he will come from far off. Unless he comes in a hundred years." She spread her hands. "If we can do no better, that is one thing, but better he wakes her in seven years. Or a year and a day if we can manage that."

The raven cawed. And cawed. And the man began to laugh.

The fairy let her breath out slowly. The man could advise the prince because the birds told him things. She should remember that.

"There's a kingdom they aren't going to," said the man. "Because it is south of the mountains."

"And the mountains are too wild to go through—usually," said the fairy in thought. "At least, without guidance."

"Then, in that kingdom, there is a king with three sons, and the king's growing, not just old, but ill," said the man.

She smiled. "This part will never make it into the tales."

"There's still work to be done. You don't want him to head into the mountains by winter, after all. Indeed, I think it will be a few years before the princes will be willing to set out on a quest to heal their father."

"We shall watch," she assured him.

Part IV

Liam walked down the street. The widest in the city, with the sky a broad ribbon of blue between the heights of the buildings, but at the moment, it was also the most full. Chickens clucking, the sweet or cracked song of vendors for their pies or starch or stockings, housewives quarreling. A messenger in livery, his letter bag over his shoulder, scowled at how hard his passage was. Gazes passed over Liam, but the familiarity that let them be sure that the blond, blue-eyed young knight was the king's youngest son meant they cared little, even when he returned after a fortnight. All the more when other things pressed the kingdom.

Two merchants, before a shop, lamented how King Stefan should have named an heir by now. Liam looked away and blinked, once. For the commons, the succession would cause the most grief. Grieving over the king's death was the place of his sons.

He walked on. He would not meet a funeral where the dead man's body lay hostage for his debts to be paid. If such a funeral were held, Kevin or Owen would have arrived and paid the debt in hopes of the dead man's ghost coming to their aid later.

His breath came out in a half laugh. He would pay it himself, with the same hope, thus removing it. It was a reward for the generous deed, not the calculation.

The castle appeared ahead. Besides, he could never spend his last penny on such an expense; he had money enough.

#

In the shadowy castle corridors, court ladies watched him, half hiding their faces with fans, or turning sideways as if to hide their faces.

His father should hold a ball for his sons to find brides, thought Liam, except that he and his brothers had met the marriageable ladies already.

Two ladies whispered. One said something about a witch's prisoner.

"She wouldn't do. If one of them married a princess, an heiress, that is the only way."

She started, as if she realized her voice carried, and blushed.

She was right, thought Liam gloomily. His father could divide the kingdom in two, the half that had come with his bride, a princess and heiress, and the half that was his own, for the other two if only one prince would marry a princess, the heiress to a kingdom. No one could object if each of them had a kingdom.

Light gleamed from the doorway ahead. Liam wondered how many candles they burned. At least they warmed the room while his father lay ill, and the doctors insisted that draft would endanger his living out the day.

For a moment, he stood in the doorway. His father did not stir. The candles filled the air with golden light, and lent his father's wax-pale face the only color that he had.

Then his father's eyes opened. Blue eyes looked at him.

Liam walked forward and knelt beside the bed.

"The robbers have been destroyed," he said.

His father coughed. "That was quick."

"It was a matter of destroying them. One—their chief if the tale is true—wooed a peasant maiden and told her to come to them."

His father coughed again.

"She arrived when they were out, and got warning to hide. And yes, the tales of their cannibalism were true. She spied on it, and then she revealed all to her village. We had only to join them in hunting them down."

His father's eyes closed. "One escaped. One always escapes."

"They stopped up all the doorways and warned their mothers and sisters of the danger—"

His father, by his breath, slept again. Liam fell silent and, when his father did not protest, stood.

It was not as if his father needed to hear. Even the mothers and sisters had rolled their eyes when warned that a bandit who seized on one of them in secret meant them ill, whatever he promised.

He walked from the room as the doctor fussed. The doctor would not, of course, breathe a word of when he expected King Stefan to die until after the king actually died. He and his brothers might hear in time to keep the death watch by the bedside for the last hours, but past that, there would be only rumors.

He walked down the corridors. Already there were rumors. If he glanced out these windows, he would no doubt see servants glancing about to discover more that they might tell their neighbors, but everyone knew King Stefan was dying. He could neither quell them nor calm those who spread them. He would have to lie to make the attempt.

At that, he would learn nothing by watching them gossip. Better to rest in the garden, with roses in bloom.

#

"Dressed to impress the princess?" said Ewan, behind him.

Liam closed his eyes. For once, Ewan had decided to come into the garden. He could only presume it was to deliver that witticism.

He felt unsurprised to find that Ewan had dressed for court, in unusual finery, and not for the road as he still was.

"Yes, of course, why aren't you ready?" said Liam, with all the cheer he could muster. "She'll arrive any minute. You shouldn't fail without trying because you are the middle son. That's unworthy of you. I won't be able to persuade the princess of silver to marry you if you don't."

Ewan's sour face was incongruously framed with delicate pink blooms. "Dressing like a gardener's boy only works when you work as a gardener's boy, in another kingdom's garden. Besides, your hair isn't *golden* enough just because it's fair. She won't sit at her window and see it when you take off your cap."

"Then it doesn't matter that I didn't go another kingdom," said Liam.

Ewan opened his mouth, but another voice said, "And how is our father?"

"Haven't you seen, Kevin?" said Liam.

Kevin walked out from another arch, with a sprinkling of fallen white rose petals on him. "The doctors don't like him to be disturbed too often. Plus, the trip away may have given you a sharper contrast."

"He's dying," said Liam.

After a minute he added, "They didn't let me stay long, and I am no judge of how long it would take."

Kevin looked as grave and sorrowful as the king's eldest son ought to be at such news. Liam, hoping he managed to look as sober, nodded to him and walked off into the rose maze. Ewan and Kevin started to talk behind him, and he took more twists and turns until it muffled the sound. His mother had always said that the maze was enchanted for silence.

He made out the sound of clipping ahead. It had to be close—

He stopped and grabbed an archway to steady himself as his wits caught up with him. "I beg your pardon. I am troubled at heart, but I should have watched where I went." Especially when he had actually heard the clipping, and not his brothers.

His heart slowed as the dwarf gardener turned his face on him. A new gardener at that. Though his cap showed his hair, which was not gold. A sober and nothing out of the ordinary brown.

The gardener pulled off his cap and bowed, as if Liam had not been staring rudely at him. "All the kingdoms know of your grief. But it seems that no one here knows of the apple that could save your father, were his sons willing to get it for him."

His heart seemed to stop. Then it seemed to hammer. He forced his voice to be steady. Unwise to be rude to anyone who might be the aid you needed for your quest, least of all to someone who seemed to know what you would need. And might have magic.

"What is happening here?" demanded Kevin, behind him, and moments later Ewan stalked after.

Liam winced. So much easier when the brothers set out separately. You would think that the dwarf would be wise enough to meet them one by one so that he could test each of them.

"Ah, three princes, three brothers, three sons of one father!"

Kevin and Ewan stopped, and their eyes narrowed. The dwarf smiled a little. His eyes danced like a well that caught a sunbeam.

"Surely this is the three-ply rope that is not easily broken! There is a way to save your father. On an apple tree in a garden in a far-off land grows fruit that can heal him."

"I must go and find this wonder!" said Kevin.

"You should stay," said Ewan. "You are the oldest son and the stay of our father. I should go."

The dwarf smiled a little, as if to say that he, too, knew the tales, and that all the sons would set out.

#

Kevin argued with the doctors all afternoon, finally triumphing by arguing that they might disrupt the king's slumber in their anxiety. At nightfall, with a single star gleaming in the deep blue sky, the three of them trooped into the chamber. The doctors fussed about. Royal councilors followed solemnly—to serve as witnesses, they insisted—and garnered more glares from the doctors.

King Stefan lay asleep. Candles burned steadily about him.

Kevin went down on his knees and took his hand. Their father opened his eyes briefly. Kevin, as if he were certainly awake, recounted the story, ignoring how his eyes closed again, and asked for leave to go.

Their father muttered something, so muddled that even Kevin, that close, could not have heard what he said. Kevin nodded, gravely, drew back his hand, and rose to his feet. The nearest candle flame shifted from his movement.

"He gave me leave," he said, brazenly, but—Liam realized—aware that no one in the room would dare give the lie to his claim. He would not do it himself. Ewan certainly would not.

"All three of you," said King Stefan with abrupt clarity.

No one moved. Liam forced himself to breathe. He looked at his father, and then at all the faces about. They had heard. No one would argue what King Stefan's position was, now.

Kevin looked sour, but he did not argue as he turned to leave. Perhaps graybeards would gripe that all three sons set out at once, rather in order, but they would do so more quietly.

And, thought Liam cheerfully, being on the road, they would not need to listen to the graybeards.

#

The tavern sign for the Wandering Bear was so faded that only memory let Liam recognize what it said. Three old graybeards with their mugs of ale sat before it in the sunlight.

A little girl, before them, looked frightened. "What if they all kill dragons and marry princesses and never return? Or fight off entire armies, or win tourneys?"

The men laughed. Liam paused.

"One will return to be King Stefan's heir," said the oldest of the three, his head bald and his white beard long. "Perhaps with a bride."

"There's nothing to fear," said the youngest, his short beard and hair showing still strands of black. "The king is not sending away his sons because they freed a prisoner, or because their wicked stepmother tricked him. It's not like any of them need to go away, except that they love their father and want to save him."

"Why, princes have been known to tell princesses they rescued from dragons that they have to leave for a year and a day. That would give the one who finds the apple time to go and return. He's not stuck in her castle."

"Isn't that always trouble? For the princess?" said the girl.

The middle one shrugged and leaned back. "Can't be helped. The king must be cured, and the princess must learn that her husband has other duties as well as to her."

The girl looked distressed.

Perhaps she would learn not to heed men merely because their beards were gray, thought Liam, striding by. The reliable ones were those you met on the road. In the woods, even.

The huntsman waiting in the tavern was another matter. He nodded to Liam, drained his mug, and rose to talk to him of the dangers of traveling through the wild woods.

A third voice rose from the graybeards, the one in the middle. "When king's sons, or anyone's sons, set out together, they part at a crossroads."

Sometimes graybeards were wise.

#

"A stupid thing to do," said Ewan. "The tree is in a *garden*. Gardens don't grow in the wild woods."

Under the stable roof, Liam looked ahead. Grooms readied the horses, but Ewan shifted around to stand before him, and glare at him.

"It's stupidity," said Ewan.

"Many a wilderness lies between gardens," said Liam. "Pines, oaks, birches, and maples, and the apples in the orchard after."

"And perhaps you can light your way through the woods by candlelight!" said Ewan. "Is there no end to your nonsense?"

"Perhaps not," said Liam.

Ewan stared at him, and the grooms brought up their horses. Liam went to mount. The sooner they left, the sooner they parted.

One stable boy muttered that one of them would feed his horse to a starving wolf, another that the wolf was less ravenous than the other boy, and they all laughed.

Liam rode. His brothers followed. Then, the older brothers never let the youngest go on a quest first. He supposed they would, indeed, part at a crossroads.

#

The horses walked briskly, but the journey would eat most of the hours of this quest. Two days in this forest, with the sky at most glimpsed in sapphire scraps between boughs that spread over the road, and no sign of human habitation until they reached the inn of a night.

Liam was seeing the point of making a magical ship that would fly over sea and land, for all the time and effort and need to befriend a magical old man.

"Crossroads ahead," called Kevin.

The ever perilous crossroads. Less danger than it could be, since they could not take the wrong road. They did not know where they were going, so they could not choose wisely—barring a stone with the warnings that to go left meant to face hunger and thirst; straight, that you would die, and your horse live; right, that you would live, and your horse die.

The right road went north, straight ahead to the west, and the left one south, but all three roads vanished into dips and hollows that were utterly hidden by the trees. Bears and witches might lie ahead, but there were no hints to show which road was perilous.

Ewan laughed. Shortly. "Of course there is not so much as a sign-post."

"And that, Ewan," said Kevin, "is why you talk to the innkeeper. To learn of crossroads ahead, and which way goes which." He turned to Liam. "They all lead to kingdoms, of course. I'll go left."

Liam nodded. If Kevin had learned where the golden apple grew, neither he nor Ewan had ever had a chance.

"I'll go straight," said Ewan, his gaze shifting from side to side.

Liam nodded again. He might as well go right. He did not even remember which kingdoms lay which way. His tutors would be ashamed of him.

He rode down the path before his brothers started down theirs. The journey would tell him what it would bring.

#

The road had already widened here. The trees had not grown so tall, and were interlaced with wild rose bushes, all in white bloom. Kevin rode through the sunshine, knowing that settled lands were soon ahead.

Liam was out as a danger. He was a fool to biddably go off into the wild woods, when looking for a fruit that grew in orchards. A taller tree cast some shade over his way. Ewan had chosen the lesser route as well. His way would reach a kingdom, but neither of his brothers had had the wits to look for a land famed for its fruit. Where better to find a magical, golden one than in it?

The roses grew more thickly, their boughs covering the roadside ditch, almost as if someone had used them as a hedge to protect the forest. What geese, thought Kevin. His horse loped along the road. Thousands of flowers abloom, abuzz with bees, and scenting the air, as if escort the hero to his prize. They had only to litter his way with flowers to make it perfect.

He came about a bend, and his horse shied, nearly throwing him into the roses, with all their thorns. After his struggle mastered it, he saw the cause: a little, brownish man, standing by the hedge, as if for the world he had the right to obstruct the way and startle horses. The little man looked up at him with dark eyes, his mouth set in wry lines as if he judged him, and not showing the slightest sign of penitence.

"What the devil are you doing, you fool?" said Kevin.

"Why, wondering what you are about, young prince?"

"About business of my own, you knave!" He slapped his heels to his horse's side, and charged onward. The manikin did not dodge, or get knocked aside, and when he glanced over his shoulder, he saw no more sign of him. Would serve him right if he died in a ditch.

A branch scratched his cheek. Kevin jerked his head away, and found leaves brushing him from the other side. He pulled up his horse, but a leaf already brushed his leg from the other side. His horse had charged into a narrow lane, so narrow that he could not turn his horse. Ahead, branches grew over the way.

He looked back. The branches were already stretching, catching him in here as if he had been fool enough to try to wake a sleeping princess.

"That thrice-accurst dwarf!"

#

Ewan rode along easily between the hedges. So much more pleasant without his brothers. He had not seen anyone for some time, but before, those he had seen had been friendly. Only prudent with a well-dressed young man on horseback.

Even more prudent than when meeting with a beggar with rags. He smirked. The danger was more immediate.

As for riding so recklessly he would nearly collide with such a beggar, he had his horse to consider. Even a genuine beggar, not just a fairy trying to pose as one to measure you in so haughty a manner, would be a danger to his horse. The princes who failed that were fools.

"Only a foolish little moon-calf would," Ewan said, and chortled. At least he was not some peasant chit who would have to work for months for some old woman to win a reward and good will. He could just not be arrogant with some beggar. Why, he could throw a beggar a pear or a loaf of bread! He had brought lunch, and enough to share. It wasn't as if older brothers had to be fools. Kevin would be, he knew, so all he had to worry about was Liam.

"Is that not so, my good man?" he caroled at a red-capped man by the crossroad, who looked back. His gaze was steady and judgmental. What a thing from a farmer to a prince. All the more in that this one was so short, couldn't win a fight even with another farmer.

"Magic is afoot, good man! Let your heart be light!"

At least the man stood by the roadside, out of the way, even if he stood oddly. A clubfoot, perhaps. The man should find his own beggar and give him his lunch. Or overhear crows talking about magical cures in the land. At least he didn't have to seek out a golden apple tree; he should be glad.

Ewan looked ahead and frowned. That oak, he had seen it before. It had an odd shape, like it had been struck by lightning and half of it was dead.

Then he shrugged. A storm that would hit one tree would hit another. He rode on, through a turn, and up a hill and down again. And then saw it again.

He scowled and looked to either hand. What fool had let the brush and oaks sprout so close to the road? Making it impossible to see through leaves? At the least, they should have put up signs at their crossroads to prevent travelers from going about in circles. No wonder so few tales spoke of peasants winning princesses, when so many spoke of princes. The princes had the judgment to win.

He kicked his horse's side, but within half an hour, he recognized the lightning blasted oak again. He had to be on a different track, he told himself, this was more overgrown than the other two times he saw it.

As if his thoughts were the words to a spell, the branches grew out, entrapping him. His horse shied at the ones before it, and tried to surge forward, and could not move. Not even to dislodge him as it shook its head.

He shifted his arm, and discovered that the brambles had thorns.

Why, that old fool who had gotten himself into a ditch! How dare he condemn a prince? He pushed, futilely, against the branches, and got himself scrapped for his pains. That wretch! He could not even keep himself out of a ditch, and he would do *this* to a prince for making a jest?

#

In the gloom, Liam let his breath out slowly. It was one thing to read about the forests in books, or even to fare among the forests of his father's lands. It was another to ride down the road, or rather path, with oaks towering round, ready for any ogre or dragon that would assail him. Though fighting would be easier than facing some disguised fairy while so unnerved.

Liam snorted. Start by not losing his way. Falling into the power of some witch, extorted when he needed her aid to leave the forest, would be worse than either. He glanced about the forest, where at least no strange and magical flower bloomed, either gold or scarlet.

His horse shied. He blinked and grabbed the reins, and looked again. An old man half lay in the ditch.

"I beg your pardon, old father." He only half realized that he had dismounted, and gotten down on one knee by the man. "Are you hurt? I was so bent on my way that I did not see you."

The old man raised an eyebrow. Between bushy eyebrows, a full beard, and a shock of white hair, it was hard to read his face. And he looked uncommonly short, even from this angle.

Liam swallowed. "I am deeply troubled at heart."

"Do you want to add to your troubles?"

"Not greatly, but if I wanted to be safe, I would never have come."
He went to help the man up. In some tales, the dwarf attacked his
helper and beat him soundly, but he had risked that peril by going on
his journey.

The old man stood easily. At least his leg was not hurt. "I had fallen
before. But there are few travelers here, and none came to aid me." He
glanced sideways at Liam. "One thinks that a traveler has to have a reason to choose this road."

"Golden apples," said Liam. His mouth was too dry for him to swal-
low again. "My father ails, and I have heard that golden apples can heal
what ails him."

"Ah, golden apples. They cure the ill, sometimes," said the dwarf.
"The land is not exactly full of them. Do you know what it is full of?"

Liam shook his head.

The dwarf leaned forward. "Soldiers."

Liam met his gaze and pondered for a moment. "A war?"

The dwarf rocked back. "Wise of you to guess so. A war. Neither
the invaders nor this kingdom's soldiers will think well of a prince who
wanders through, looking for golden apples."

"I thank you for your counsel, I do not doubt your word, but I must
go on, whatever the danger. My father ails, and no doctor can aid him."
He drew a deep breath. "Is there a way that would be wisest to go and
find the apples?"

The dwarf smiled a little. "There's a castle up in the mountains. Better yet, you do not have go far into the kingdom at war. The castle may
look as if only a cat could get into it—" He cast Liam another sideways glance. "—but do not judge too much by appearances. Inside that
castle, there is a garden. Inside that garden, there is a tree. And in the
boughs of that tree, there are golden apples. And going that way will let
you evade most of the soldiers." The dwarf smiled and waved his hand
at the slope. "All of them, if you take care."

That, at least, was no surprise. "Is there anything particular I should do to evade the soldiers, or find the castle?"

"Be courteous to those you meet. And look for a castle covered with roses."

Liam stood silent for a moment longer and then, when the dwarf said no more, courteously thanked him, wished him Godspeed, and rode on.

#

The forest went on for days. He did not meet two more little men by the road with more advice, but then, he did not met soldiers, either. Once, he hid in the forest, only to watch a woodcutter, burdened with a great bundle of wood, go by.

He did not come out hiding until the man had gone on. It would not do to grow complacent. The closer he came, the more likely there were to be soldiers.

Now, as he came about a turn, the forest opened up and showed him the slope.

A great mass of roses stood ahead. He almost thought he could smell it, at this distance. They engulfed an entire hill, or castle, covering it with colors like a sunset. Not wild roses, and it did look—he smiled—as if a cat could get into it.

A small village clustered about it, and figures moved about. Most of whom would be children, women, or old men, he knew, though he could not see at this distance.

It was noon. He should not wait for tomorrow.

#

The road wound more than he had thought it would, but he still arrived in the village by daylight. The graveyard did not seem to have many new graves, but indeed, few young men were about.

He wondered whether they had taken to the wild or been taken into the army.

At that, there were few enough people. Some clearly saw him and edged, or hurried, off.

But the castle was clear enough. What else could bear that great mass of roses? And not the sweet, lovely, but tiny wild roses that would grow hither and yonder and make shepherds curse that they took over the pasture. Great enormous blooms in scarlet and delicate pink and peach. Close up, it still looked as if a sunset had hidden on the hilltop.

Or a sunrise. He could hope for a sunrise, no doubt.

He rode toward the castle and eyed the roses. No bones could be seen among them. He wondered if perhaps he was the first prince here as he rode into the castle's shadow. This close, he could make out the shape of the building below, but on the cool air, the sweet scent of the roses abounded more than a perfumer's shop. The roses nodded as bees alighted, hard at work. Liam called to mind what the dwarf had said. A prince who ignored such words deserved no help. He dismounted and tied his horse to the sturdiest bush, and it began to graze. He would save his father by punctiliously obeying the instructions, and thanking Heaven he did not need to ignore a golden cage for a plain wooden one.

First, he had to find the door, and pray Heaven that he could open it. He walked closer and eyed the dense roses and the stone behind it. Birds twittered, and young fledglings hopped from branch to branch, their nests abandoned beyond them. He walked along, and his gaze went up and down the wall, and he realized, to his surprise, that he saw an opening. A door stood in a nook, within strides, and he had only to brush by the roses to reach it.

For a moment, he feared that the roses would move and grab him, but he reached the door without a scratch. Enchanted, perhaps, to let him in. He pulled it shut behind him and turned to face the castle.

Inside, the dim light was greenish, everywhere, but the place looked commonplace enough. He had seen hunting lodges before. If this one was sparse in the trophies, it still held the rooms and corridors, and the rough wood that they fancied.

Dust was everywhere, light and very even, like a veil. Cobwebs here and there.

Gardens, now, were uncommon in hunting lodges, but the most likely place was the center. Liam set out briskly. A hunting lodge would not have its corridors set out in elegant order, to impress all who visited with the dignity of the royal court, but it would hardly be a labyrinth.

A point he reminded himself of, after he found the kitchen, and realized it had only one entrance not covered with roses. He turned and went back. His footsteps echoed from the kitchen's flagstones, and the corridor ahead looked much like the others he had walked down. Was he quite, quite sure that it was not a labyrinth?

He yawned. Then he blinked. It was broad daylight, however green. He had no excuse to be sleepy, and at that, no servants slept, here or there, not so much as a dog or a cat. The kitchen's hearth had been brushed clean of ash, not holding a sleeping fire.

Still he yawned again.

Liam scowled for a moment. He would have thought that the dwarf would have warned him of any enchantment that would put him to sleep. The dwarf hadn't so much as warned him that he had to leave before midnight.

Still, he walked faster.

Light grew brighter, ahead of him, and he walked faster still, not quite willing to break into a run.

This corridor also ended in a chamber. Windows let sunlight pour through, though the room was large enough that much of it lay in shadow. In the center, below the window, stood the bed, with its sumptuous bed curtains, royal blue with golden crowns, and about, in the shadows, the furnishings were finely wrought wood, sometimes gilt. He swallowed. This was a hunting lodge bed chamber, and for that, it was fit for royalty.

He shifted about, to look out. The windows opened on a garden. Through the leaded panes he could see flowers nodding in a breeze, and trees. His breath came out with an abruptness that startled him. One tree's leaves, shifting in the breeze, showed fruit that flashed golden when sunlight struck it.

Fully ripe, and yet not a fruit had fallen from the tree. That was more magical than the golden color. He started across the room, taking care for his footing in the shadows, and his gaze went across the shadowed depths of the bed.

There lay a maiden no older than he was.

He froze where he stood. A radiantly lovely maiden, her brown hair and rosy pink skirt spilling over the blankets, asleep in a castle where no one had walked for months, if not years, next to an enchanted garden, behind enchanted roses. . . .

After a moment, he inched over to the bedside. When she did not stir, he pulled back the curtain. The sunlight fell on the blankets without rousing her from her sleep. Her cheeks were rosy, and her lips were as red as roses, and a prince must think of rescuing the enchanted maiden, not devising poems like some love-sick minstrel.

When he, holding his breath in doubt, lowered his hand to her mouth, her warm breath flowed over his hand. His own breath gushed out. He did not even have to find a mirror.

Though a mirror he could question would help.

He looked about. In a musty corner, a mirror reflected his pale face, and Liam grimaced. He was no witch, to enchant it to answer him.

More prudent to hire a cart and lug her off, and drop her to see if it would dislodge a bit of apple from her throat. Which was also folly. She did not lie in a coffin. Remember your tales, he told himself. No spindle and distaff lay in her grip, and so he took up her hands, trying to notice whether anything marred them, even so much a bit of flax under a nail.

They were flawless.

He lowered her hands back to the bed, and his mouth drew into a line. There was one way left. She lay as if ready to wake up at a word, but she would not.

He bent over the bed and kissed her rosy mouth.

He straightened slowly, but she did not stir. Her breathing was unchanged, her eyes did not flicker, and his face started to burn. A hundred princes could die in the thorns before the right one arrived to wake the princess. He should praise Heaven that the roses here did not kill.

He jerked away from the bed, stumbling over a stool and knocking it sprawling. His breath light and fast, he looked about the room. The windows were large, leading to the garden, but—the flower beds outside were filled with bushes, not flowers, and there was no door to the garden.

He turned away. The mirror showed his face burning red, and he fled, out the door, and down the corridor, testing every door until he stumbled into the garden.

With the sunlight shining on him, he drew a deep breath. The tree stood ahead. The leaves shaded the golden fruit, but sunlight danced through the gaps and made the fruit gleam. He walked up, reminding himself that he had come for this, for his father's sake.

He carefully eyed the boughs, to pick a good apple, and saw an eye as dark as soot look back at him. He blinked, it blinked, and he picked out the bird, as large as a pheasant, its fiery feathers more brilliant in the shade than the apples in the sun.

With sweet notes, it leapt the air, tearing through the leaves, and flew off, gleaming like a coal.

A firebird, of course. Liam smiled a little. He was not there to see that it did not steal all the apples, or to bring it back to his father. The dwarf had not advise him to bring it safely back in the plain cage, not the golden.

Memory stabbed. He drew a deep breath. When the prince ignored that, he ended up returning not only with a firebird, but a horse of power and a princess as well. He already knew he would not return with the princess. He was helpless to break the curse on her.

He eyed the nearest apple. It looked sound, it felt solid under his fingers, and he picked it. It felt like any apple did, in his hand. Carefully, he stored it away.

He stood a minute longer, calculating a way outside that did not lead past the princess. He had time enough to flee this castle and this village before nightfall. The villagers would be happier that way.

#

"So unkind."

The voice was sweet, feminine, and indifferent. Kevin bit his lip. He and his horse were both streaked from red where the thorns had scratched them bloody, and she was discourteous, but no one but a fool would speak rashly to someone who could come into these branches.

"I give you good day, my lady."

Laughter followed. "Here I thought that courtesy had died out in the land! To be so hailed by a man himself so bloodied and injured!"

"I would bow, my lady," he said, with more confidence, "could I move."

The branches pulled back.

Not too far. The branches still held his horse in place, and he could hardly dismount and flee.

Her meaning was clear enough. He bowed in the saddle. This was no insolent dwarf meanly feigning to be some ignoble fellow and expecting to be treated as a noble, but a forthright fairy, showing her power and her claim to his respect.

Apparently the bow was deep enough. The branches withdrew from his way, and his horse snorted and walked forth. Kevin kept a careful watch and drew the horse up as soon as he saw her. She gleamed in gold like sunlight.

He bowed again. She could toss him about like a rag doll if she felt inclined. Which gave him hope of aid. Surely a woman who could command thorn bushes could find a tree with golden apples that could heal his father, and win him the kingdom as his inheritance.

His heart began to beat, not faster, but harder. Courtesy, he reminded himself. She would not object to his untidiness, after his long journey, but he had to be as courteous as his tongue could be.

"Already I am deeply in your debt, my lady."

She smiled. But flattery alone would not win her over to his side. So fair and lovely a lady would hear much, and merit it too.

Offer her no aid, he reminded himself.

"Alas, I long to linger, but I am bound to a quest for my dear father's sake. He ails, and I must find a golden apple to save his life—" He stared.

Against her golden gown, her hand bore a gold apple.

"Perhaps if the dwarf had not thwarted you," she murmured, "you would have it already. How I hate false dealing." She leaned forward. "Perhaps if your brother had not tricked you to this path, you would have it already."

Kevin blinked. "I choose my path."

"So crafty of him. No doubt he has convinced you that he is all but simple."

Her smile deepened. He felt the color drain from his face. Then abruptly, he realized what Liam must have done. "The knave!" His hand formed a fist, and his face must be fiery with rage. "He—he—"

The lady, still smiling, waited until his rage had sunk. Then she held up her hand.

"This is a false apple," said the lady, delicately.

He blinked. Thinking on that was calming. She meant something by giving him that.

"Were it to replace the true apple, no one would notice." She shifted it in her hand, sending sunlight glinting this way and that. "Until the king ate it. And a treacherous brother might be dealt his due, that way."

#

Ewan yawned. He could fall over and scratch his eyes out. He glared at the thorns about him. That would be shocking. He had not met a beautiful maiden, imprisoned in a tower by a wicked witch. His eyes should not be poked out by thorns.

He yawned again.

"What a shame. When I want to offer you a sleeping potion."

His eyes popped open. A woman stood outside the thorns, dressed in violet, smiling a little. She held a bottle.

His heart pounded. He was saved! —if he won her over. But really, she must have seen the dwarf and realized how monstrously he had been treated. He was well placed, he had won her already by his sufferings and the injustice done him.

Though he should be civil, he supposed.

"I'd bow, most gracious lady, except that it's awkward here."

She laughed like chiming bells. The thorns fell back from him. He gave his very deepest bow in return.

"So courteous," she said. "So very courteous."

It was almost embarrassing to find that all those annoying tutors had told the truth. Still, having made the right impression, he should use it.

"But, my lady, I must wonder why you offer me a sleeping potion. Surely you do not mean me to put myself to sleep to await a princess? That is so hard on the princess, when she must wake the prince! She never can just take a spindle from his hands, or a sword, or kiss him—she must sit by his bed for three years, three months, three weeks, three days and three hours, and always some ugly impostor tricks her in the last hour."

"You will insist that your bride be beautiful?"

"An impostor is never of good character," said Ewan, delicately. He closed his mouth carefully before observing that such an ugly impostor was never enchanted, either, to be broken of her ugliness. Not that he wanted the effort of disenchanting one, but it would be as bad to have to work out that the beautiful woman was the one he should really marry to the satisfaction of all the court.

"Ah, how true." She put a finger to her lip. "For instance, a brother who pretends that his oldest brother choose their ways, when he tricked him, and his next older brother, into the wrong ways, because he thought merely being the youngest entitled him to the throne."

He started to laugh. That foolish Liam? Tricking Kevin? He could not trick the court fool, that solemn, over-serious fool.

The lady, her fingers wrapped around a bottle, smiled serenely. His laughter died away. In the silence after, he pondered tales of peasant boys who hid their wits while they sat in the cinders.

A breeze rustled the leaves. It was, he supposed, as possible for a prince to show as much craft as a peasant. Especially a sly one, who feigned virtue to win over the king.

"Look at you," she said softly. "You will return in rags and patches, when you set out so boldly. He won't."

She held out the bottle. "It holds a sleeping potion. You may find a use for it. But you should hurry back, now. It may rain, and you do not want to fall ill when you must be alert to treachery."

With great care, he took it. He must indeed. Treachery should be served with treachery.

#

Rob watched the pool with narrowed eyes, though it once again showed the trees about. "It seems clear enough."

"If you think we need to act this early," said the Fairy of Pine Tree Falls, "I wish I had had the wits to set a spell to know the path he traced in detail."

The dwarf sat back on his heels and raised an eyebrow. "You had a plan?"

"Within a week, it will be safe to go into the castle. She will still be asleep, but the spell will not catch us even though we are not princes." She shook her head. "It nearly caught him, and before he broke the spell. We do not have his safety—but a week should do it."

"Too late." Rob shook his head. "He will have met his brothers by then."

"It's not as if there were much you could do to warn him. I assure you, I did all I could to see how *they* spoke to them."

"Warn him that his brothers have evil hearts." The dwarf stood. "It is traditional, and we did not have time enough to see whether this one has good wits. We'll have to learn now."

#

The forest closed about Liam like a guard, and his breath came out in a gush. The soldiers might still reach him, from armies that lost their way or men who deserted their commanders, but he still felt glad to leave the kingdom that was at war.

He did not look back. At that, he left with the apple he sought. He should not blame himself for not saving a princess when he had no reason to think that he could. That curse would break in its own time, no doubt.

He rode on.

A little man stood by the road, surprising him. He pulled up his horse, and grew certain that it was the same one. He had obeyed the directions and obtained the apple. Did the dwarf think to test him again?

Losing his temper would be the most perfect folly. It was one thing to be courteous when seeking advice, but a prince ought to be courteous when he needed nothing. He winced. Then, a prince ought to be able to wake an enchanted princess from her sleep.

He reminded himself, sharply, to attend to what was before him. It would distract, at least.

And a prince ought to remember, by this point, to be grateful to a benefactor.

"Good evening, my good man," he said. At least he would not fail such a test. "I give you thanks for the good you have done me."

The dwarf snorted before saying, "Good evening, my young prince. I come bearing a warning."

Liam nodded slowly, watching.

"Beware your brothers. They do not mean you well."

Liam felt a prick of annoyance. What sensible youngest son would trust his older brothers, so prone to slither like poisonous snakes and win the prize?

Still, he nodded gravely. "I would not want my tutors to be ashamed of my studies. But—is there more reason to suspect them than that they are my older brothers?"

The dwarf gave him a sideways glance. "Now, if it were that easy to be wise to the ways of elder brothers, they would never succeed in their plots, now, would they?"

Liam said, "It won't be possible to get ahead of them if I ride hard, will it?"

The dwarf shook his head.

#

Ewan ordered their dinner, and by the evening sunshine, Kevin glared at the table, ungratefully. Meager fare for two king's sons, and without even the apple to recompense them. He wondered if Ewan had done all that he could have. Perhaps they were lucky to get chicken for the soup, though they could have gotten better at the castle. Without having to deal with Liam's treachery.

All the more reason to treat with each other prudently.

"Dwarfs," Kevin muttered.

"They are a nuisance," said Ewan. "Fairy ladies are better."

Kevin turned his head to face him. Ewan looked back, a fatuously content fool, as if he did not even notice what their meal was like. He would have to tell the truth to winkle out his story. He forced his breath in and out. She *had* said that Liam had betrayed them both. If there were any chance to pay Liam back, Ewan might aid him, but he would need proper guidance to do it properly. Do it wrong, and Ewan would worsen the matter.

"Just our bad luck, that Liam didn't find a house built by a witch out of candy and treats," growled Kevin. "While she was looking for her dinner."

"Not bread?" said Ewan.

Kevin barked a laugh. "As if any prince would find that tempting!"

"If he were lost in the forest long enough," said Ewan. "But that would require more good luck than we have."

Kevin sat back and scowled. Ewan started to eat.

Kevin, with a sigh, picked up his cup. "True enough. Consulting a forester before he left. He knew that he would go into a forest."

Kevin eyed Ewan as a maid would eye a hearth, trying to guess whether more firewood was needed. He would have to deal with Ewan after, for this mistrust and his will to seize the kingdom.

"Wiser to discuss it over dinner, and not wait for lunch," said Ewan. "The servants care less to overhear it than Liam would. He would look for it, anyway." He drank his cider. "And it would be folly to leave without him. Why, we might be accused of murder."

Kevin looked at him with narrowed eyes. Ewan shrugged. If they did not agree, well, the last thing he wanted was a reed growing on Liam's grave to pipe that Kevin had killed him, and Ewan was guiltless. He sat back.

"Do you know what the golden apple looks like?" said Kevin, coldly.

"It's an apple," said Ewan. "And gold."

"It looks like this."

Little though the light in tavern was, the apple gleamed in Kevin's
hand. Ewan gawked and gabbled something about a fairy lying.

"Oh, if I gave this to our father, I would rue the day. So would you."
He put the apple away again, before a servant saw it. "But—if Liam
handed *this* to our father, our father will never speak his name again."
Kevin's tongue touched his lips. Would Ewan actually help in figur-
ing out how to change them? Either to attempt or to be useful? Some
middle brothers stole the throne without even finding the golden apple or slaying the dragon—merely by ineffectually trying to protect the
youngest from the eldest. Kevin glanced sideways at him. Certainly he
should not mention that it might hasten the hour of his inheritance.

The golden apple—Liam's golden apple—would fix that. And their
father had to eat it, or there would be no way to show it was the true
one.

As fatuous as ever, missing all the complications before them, Ewan
smiled. "And I have a means to secure that." He pulled out the bottle,
and explained it briefly. Kevin smiled himself. To be sure, he had to ensure that Ewan did not steal the false apple, but that was a risk he had
to take; Ewan would ensure he could not steal the water, he had wits
enough for that.

"At the next inn, we must order a roast duck," said Ewan. "Or at
least a roast chicken. To celebrate."

"No," said Kevin. As if they could count on being able, but more
than that— "No counting our chicks unhatched. We will have time
enough for banquets with roast peacock, once Liam's treachery is dealt
with. We must be ready to move."

#

The day was superb, brilliantly blue, and would have been all the better if his brothers had not waited for him at the crossroads.

"Did either of you get a spyglass so that we could see how our father fares?" said Liam. "Or at least a flying carpet?"

They both gave him baneful glares, and he cursed himself. The three brothers who gained three equal things, the third of which was an apple that could cure illness—reminding them was unwise.

He managed to smile and disclaim either thing, but neither one grew cheerful. He suggested that the inn was still hours away, and all three of them turned to the road.

"I trust you avoided wars," said Liam.

Kevin gave him a sidelong glance. "You don't look like you fought in one."

"I managed to avoid so much as seeing a battlefield, let alone a battle." Liam shook his head. "But there was war in the land where I went. You could see it in all the young men who weren't there."

Among the wildflowers that filled the ditch, a bee buzzed. He shook his head. "But this is no time to stand and gossip. Our return is no doubt awaited hourly, or at least daily."

#

The hard riding left them stained with dirt, and Kevin waved his hand to pull back Ewan from the inn, and the wash water. As if dealing with Liam was so urgent it required they be filthy while they talked.

"Did you notice how he never reached for that pouch on his belt? As if he were distracting us?"

Ewan raised an eyebrow.

"We could get it while he washed."

And leave you with no debt to me? thought Ewan. "No, the fairy did not give me the potion without a good reason for it. Do not reject her advice. As foolish as taking the golden cage when the fox told you to take the plain one."

He wished he had not told Kevin. If he merely took the apple and rushed ahead, he could cure their father, and no one would question who merited the reward of their father's kingdom. Now, both he and Kevin might lay claim, if Kevin did not get ahead of him.

"We will do it tonight, that will help her magic."

#

Liam woke abruptly, far past dawn. Sunlight cast beams into the room, warming it to uncomfortable heat, and he heard nothing of his brothers. The rats, he thought without thinking, and his hand went to check the apple. It was still there.

Perhaps they had met princesses and gone back to woo, said an impish piece of folly.

As if either Kevin or Ewan would bother to return with a prospect of a kingdom in hand, or woo a princess without one! He shoved back the covers and rose.

The innkeeper jovially assured that he had drunk as for a festival, and his brothers had left him to sleep it off because he would not be roused. He said nothing. He had not drunk enough to forget drinking less than usual and telling Kevin and Ewan that he would go to bed early given his hard day's travel. He wondered how much they had paid the man to lie, but he had need of haste.

He rode off and asked along the way, but no one remembered his brothers having ridden along the road. Perhaps they had offended a dwarf and been caught in brambles, or turned to stone, even this close to their return, but he had never heard of such a tale.

He heard no word of his brothers before the castle rose into view.

Reaching the castle, he reminded himself, had been his aim all along. Even asking about his brothers had wasted time that should have been spent riding hard on the journey. Unkempt as he was, he should go directly to his father.

Liam rode up. Grooms and stable boys scrambled out—to get the news, he suspected—but they took his horse. Servants milled about but left his way clear in haste. Liam went from room to room, courtiers pulling from his way without even trying to speak to him, his footsteps often ringing more loudly than ever before, but he could not slow now.

At the end of a long corridor, filled with slanting sunbeams and lazily drifting motes of dust, the door to his father's chambers appeared ahead. He swallowed. How far he had fared, and yet the end was in sight. He could not run within the castle, but he walked faster. The servant did not have time to reach the door to before he opened it himself.

The doctors must have gone for the day, to pother over their books and their medicines. A small, timid maidservant sat by the bed, and within it lay his father, so still and worn and pale that Liam did not wonder that the doctors had forborne to poke at him.

Servants already peeked about the open door, and from the chatter, someone had sent word ahead. He had never been so gawked at, or heard so many whispers. Not one of which mattered. He knelt by the bed and drew out the apple. It gleamed gold in the bedroom. He was not entirely certain whether it glowed only by sunlight, but then, he had not sought it to light his way.

Whispers grew louder.

His father shifted a little. His eyes opened a crack, and then they popped open, and he stared at the apple. It reflected in his eyes.

He coughed. "Where are your brothers?"

"I have not seen them," said Liam. True enough, not since the day before. When his father did not speak again, he said, "We went by different paths from a crossroad." That, too, was true enough. The inn had been at a crossroads. And if they had not gone by a different path this morning, well, they had gone by different roads to find the apple, or not.

That was nothing. Now he had to heal his father.

"Should I cut the apple for you?" he said.

His father gave a little laugh. "I can eat an apple yet, my son."

"Should I help you up? Or have the servants do it? I know they must be better at shifting you after these sad months."

Two menservants were beside the bed, moving pillows, before the words had quite finished. His father sat.

For an insane moment, Liam dreaded handing over the apple. His brothers were untrustworthy, and they had left him.

But his father was dying.

He held it out. His father took the apple in hand, and bit.

The apple crumbled into black dust against the teeth, for a brief moment appearing as a black, hollow shell before it crumbled entirely into his father's lap, and his mouth.

Liam gaped.

His father stared at him for a ghastly moment before collapsing on the pillows, whiter than the sheets, and the menservants, terror and horror on their faces, raised their hands as if to grab him.

"Quick!" Kevin's voice resounded. "If we are not in time to catch Liam, we must be in haste to save King Stefan." He ran into the chamber, Ewan following. "Get him away from the king!"

Ewan pulled out a golden apple. That one did glow, more brightly than the sunlight. Their father looked all the more ill by the light.

A manservant started to grab Liam's arm.

Liam turned and fled. The startled manservant's hand missed, and Liam took the door to the garden, and there into the maze.

Moments later, he heard the cries of elation from the castle, and did not linger to hear orders to pursue him. He fled through the maze, picking his ways with care, knowing soldiers and servants knew the maze as well as he did. Once he stopped, his heart hammering, his breath harsh, as he realized the next corner would bring him face to face with soldiers.

In the moment, he remembered—a hiding place was near here. He had hidden there as a small boy, and—he had to risk it. As softly as he could, he stole down the path and squeezed into a corner that had been less thorny when he had been smaller.

There he crouched, his breath growing easier and his heart slowing. He felt vaguely grateful that he had walked in straight from the way to his father, still in his travel clothes. The dirt on drab clothes could only help in his hiding.

"Oh, he won't be fool enough to hide down that way, it's a dead end," said a servant, sharply. "Don't waste your time, he'll get away."

Liam's shoulders slumped in relief. His heartbeat slowed again. Thank Heaven for blessing him with even this brief safety. He listened for footsteps. None came his way.

He waited. And waited. Nebulous plans of escape came and went as he forced himself to patience.

When church bells rang the hour, he stirred. Slowly, he emerged from the thicket and its thorns not that much more bloodied after going in. His head bowed, he walked down the maze's paths.

He did not stumble on another dwarf as a gardener. He flinched at the memory, but three visits were the most he could expect. He reminded himself that he did not have to go that far for the gate that let him flee into the forest.

He watched carefully as he approached the gate. No one was near. The last thing he needed was the news that he had gotten free, to the forest, where he could flee in any direction.

But he saw no one, and heard no one. The gate opened at a touch.

Once in the shade of the trees, he let his breath out. He could eat his trail food on the way, and it would savor more than any royal feast.

But first he needed distance from the castle. About the hill, past the stream, and into the grove of birches.

There, fortune failed him. Three foresters looked at him in surprise. His breath came too fast even for the distance he had fled.

The oldest, his hair so grizzled that it was nearly as pale as it was dark, lifted an eyebrow. "Did your father order us to take you out into the depths of the forest and kill you in secret?"

The youngest snorted. "They don't tell the *prince* that."

The third said, his voice kindly, "Don't look so shocked, Your Highness. We knew that your brothers are not the type to offer to cut off the head of the talking fox because it demands it, and you can not bring yourself to do it."

"I was a fool," said Liam. "The dwarf warned me to not trust them, and I did not tell them anything, but—I traveled with—"

The middle one raised his hand. "And now you must travel without them."

"At least you are already dressed for the road," said the youngest.

"Without looking so much like a prince that strangers will take you for one," said the oldest.

Just as well, thought Liam. He would be lucky to find a job as a scullion. He collected himself enough to thank them.

"There will be little enough we can do for you," said the youngest.

#

Firs cast deep shadows over the path and the forest floor, covered with amber needles and bearing not a single plant beneath the boughs.

The foresters had been very generous with him, Liam reminded himself. They had no doubt gone hungry that day when they gave him their food. He tried to not remember that he had felt hungry for the week he managed to eke out those meals, and now he would go hungry indeed.

Heaven help him. He bowed his head and trudged on. The path had risen for the last three days.

It was hard to be grateful for the path now. He had actually thought it good when they brought him to a little used path, thinking he would meet few travelers who could betray him. He had met none—and found nothing. Though it kept him from going about in circles, a little used path went where few cared to go.

Firs gave way to a stand of pale birches, and sunlight flooded about, pale green through the leaves. The trees were large enough that they stood far apart. Between them, ferns grew thickly, and sometimes brushed him on either side as he walked onward. His pace did not vary.

He wondered whether he should hope to meet with an ancient man who could summon all the animals in the world, and find nothing to help him, and send him on to his still more ancient brother who could summon all the fish in the world.

Which would not help. Not even the third, the most ancient, brother, who could summon all the birds in the world. What question could he ask them?

Where to find a position, or just a meal, he supposed. He did not have the money he had borne with him on his journey for the apple, and this journey would last longer. He ran a hand through his hair. Perhaps he could ask the way to another princess, one whom he could save.

He looked over the slope ahead. No cottage stood to be seen from the way, but something moved through the trees, too ruddy in shade to be a deer.

Unless it was a strange, enchanted deer. Perhaps a doe that was, in truth, a fair princess enchanted.

He hesitated, and the creature lumbered into a clearing. Sunlight shone all about the chestnut-colored—bear. A large bear, far larger than he. It sniffed the air, and turned its head toward him.

Liam's hand went out to touch a birch trunk, beside him.

The bear sniffed the air.

Liam was up the tree before he had time to realize what he was doing. He had reached rather flimsy boughs, but he did not even think of descending. His breath steadied, and his heart slowed, but neither one absolutely as the bear ambled forward. It paused beneath the tree, looking up and sniffing.

It stood up, put its paw to the trunk, and pushed.

A little, tentatively, and not a hammer blow, but Liam had no doubt whatsoever that the bear could have down the tree on a moment.

"An unkindly greeting," said the bear, its voice human if growling. It looked up the tree. "Your coming down would make any fight easier for you."

Liam swallowed. At least it spoke to him. Slowly, he descended, finding the footing harder to find than when he climbed, but still he stood on the ground before the bear more swiftly than he dreamed possible. It settled to the ground and stood on all fours, and still came to his shoulder.

"And what is a handsome young prince doing on this way?"

Liam swallowed. No one had recognized him as a prince except the dwarf. Then, the bear could talk. "I am looking for a position. I can garden, or work as a scullion."

"Without a cap to hide your hair?"

Liam swallowed again. He did not have the gold hair that a runaway prince might hide under a cap, but then, that prince had freed a wild man from imprisonment, not tried—and failed—to save his father, and tried—and failed—to free a princess from a curse. "Tales from of old can warn of what can happen, but they can not decree it."

"Then, perhaps, a prince might take a position not at a king's castle, but a bear's."

#

The garden was small, enclosed with walls where moss grew, and mostly contained sweet roses in red and white.

The bear had not mentioned that he had no daughter, either, but—Liam drove his spade into the ground—he had the position he sought.

It was not as if he could turn into a valiant knight leading a force of knights to save the bear's kingdom from an army, though it was peopled like other kingdoms, and had servants besides him.

He wiped his forehead and turned to the new rosebush. He could be glad that he had not found a wizard living alone in the woods who could turn him into a bear. That would end badly.

At least, though it took many minutes to do it properly, he had a rose bush of pure white blooms planted and watered and sitting in sunlight but sheltered from the wind. That at least was well done.

Part V

The room was gray with dust, with evening, and with shadow. No spiders spun webs, and over the bed, the air was so still that the only blanket was the literal one that Rosaleen lay on.

The fairy pulled her skirts up and wondered whether they should have come. The enchantment was somewhat delicate.

"The garden looks different at least," said one dwarf, she did not notice which one. It was said softly, at least, and their voices were soft as they all agreed that that was good, midsummer and not autumn at all, and then they peered at Rosaleen and wondering how long it would take, and whether they could really judge.

"He's long gone, and has had time to get away," grumbled Ellen. Then she sneezed. The sound resounded, louder than their voices.

All the dwarfs started and stared at Rosaleen, who did not stir.

"We can't let her find us walking about," said Ned. "It would give all away. Ordinary people don't wake and walk about under the enchantment."

"All the more," said Adam, "in that the villagers will say that we were not about the village while she slept." He shook his head.

"She knows that the prince entered without being a fairy or dwarf," said the fairy. "True, it might be best. She'll have questions enough about your being outside. But for now—"

She walked up to the mirror. "Mirror, mirror, on the wall, show the prince who heard the call."

Ellen snorted. "Oh, that's good." But even she was silenced when the mirror began to mist over. Then it cleared. They watched as the prince entered, through the kiss, to his departure in despair.

"He's unhappy," said Rob, and the others rolled their eyes. It was a curse, after all. "And I worked it out. If she wakes today, it will have been seven years, seven months, seven weeks, and seven days!"

Ellen snorted. "It could have been a century and a day. We did well to speed it up."

Then Rosaleen sighed.

It did not take four heartbeats before all the dwarfs, and the fairy as well, were gone, and the mirror was just a mirror again.

#

She yawned. And then she sneezed. Too much dust. . . except that her room was faithfully dusted. . . and the sunlight had changed. . . which it would have if she slept. . . but then—she sat up to be certain—the garden had changed, too.

Rosaleen rose to her feet. Dust lay thin and fine over everything. Nothing in the room had been destroyed, or suffered harm, and the garden outside flourished, but the flowers nodding in the breeze were brilliant with color, and blooming far later in the year than they should have.

Should have if she had just napped for a few hours. That the curse had fallen would explain all. She knew they had not bloomed when she had lain down. Dust, garden, silence. . . .

She swirled about, and dust flew. She coughed, and as the dust began to settle, her heart hammered. She had not deceived the dwarfs, ever, about the danger they were in—she had not so much as hinted by holding her tongue that her curse was other than what it was—but that felt a weak staff to lean on. She did not know how long she, and everyone else, had slept.

She glanced at the wardrobe, but the summer had yet to grow much hotter. She could wear this gown while she learned. She picked her way about the room, trying to avoid rousing the dust, and wondered if the fires had slept, or if a boiling pot had boiled in the kitchen until the water had boiled away and the pot had been ruined.

At least there were only the dwarfs, she told herself, and tried avoid rejoicing over. Then she realized that perhaps some had been outside, and watched while others slept. She winced. Inside or outside for all, she hoped Heaven granted that. Or else a very short sleep for her. Perhaps no more than the months to this season—

She stopped and forced her breath in and out. If she had awoken centuries later, so that all the folk about found her quaint, she had at least been woken by a prince. She should collect her thoughts before her quest, and she had one way to judge the time. She looked out the window.

The plants in the garden had not grown that much, she told herself, and swallowed. Her sleep could not have been too long, or the entire castle would have been overgrown. The garden bore many weeds, she could see them from here, and some flowers had vanished. Many flowers had vanished. Only those that reseeded, or overwintered, blossomed. She forced her breath in and out. The gardeners had always favored those, for ease, and so it had not turned completely into a wilderness of rank weeds, with all the lovely flowers choked out.

At that, the flowers still grew, more or less, where they had been planted. Still, it was wiser to go by the trees.

From the way the trees had grown, she had not slept for a few months.

Horn, she reminded herself. And handkerchief. She needed those things. Everything else in the castle she could spare, but the horn and the handkerchief could not be replaced. She turned back to the room to find them in the satchel, which did not fall apart at the touch.

These reflections did not calm her. She took up the satchel just in case, and the leather was still as supple as if she had napped. Rosaleen let her breath out. Perhaps she should go into the garden and contemplate flowers and bees. She would think better in a peaceful frame.

The mirror showed her face, and it was not lack of sunlight that made her so pale. She should stop playing the timid little mouse.

"Mirror, mirror, on the wall, show me the prince, and what did befall."

Her face remained. It did not even blur a little.

There, she told herself. She needed to find out herself. She should see what happened to the dwarfs, first, and perhaps to the villagers. Duty before peace. Especially for a princess.

They might have news, at that. She went to the door and pushed it open. The dust lay smooth on the corridor.

She stepped outside, and heard voices, which drove all other thoughts from her mind. She ran down the way, her footsteps echoing, and moments later, as she burst into the kitchen, she saw the dwarfs. They turned their faces toward her, and they all, even Ellen, smiled broadly.

"Here you are! All bright and cheerful!" Tom threw his hands in the air.

"Ready to disguise yourself as an actor in a troupe, so we can sneak about?" called Molly.

"That would be silly, we would not be safe on the road as mere play actors," said Ned.

Molly shrugged. "We could move about freely that way."

"Get moved along as undesirable," said Ellen.

"We do want to move along," said Adam, his voice conciliatory. "And if they do it too harshly, well, the princess can summon some soldiers."

"Not too many," said Rosaleen, firmly, hoping to squelch. "I can't send them back afterwards. They would eat."

"All the more reason to earn some coins," said Molly. "For food."

Amy rolled her eyes. "We have coins. We serve the princess. We have the treasure sent to us to feed her." She waved a hand in the air. "Our problem is seeming poor enough for our clothes and the littleness of our company."

The dwarfs pondered that, and in the silence, a bird sang outside the window.

"At least you didn't sleep so long that there are no longer troupes of players," said Adam, pertly.

"We would move faster," said Amy, "if we just went as travelers. A family, and—" A sidelong glance at Rosaleen. "—another who joined for safety in number."

"If we can find clothes that will make the story plausible," said Rosaleen. A bit primly. Her tongue touched her lips. "I wore my own clothes to fetch the horn, but—I don't think that would be prudent here." They looked at her, and she felt her cheeks growing warm. "I did go to another kingdom then—"

Tom snorted. "Just across the border and nothing more. You were right then that nothing more was needed, and you are right now that we need actual disguises here."

"True, true," said Molly. "We will need clothing for you to appear common and nondescript, and clothing for you to appear as a princess traveling, and clothing for you to appear as a princess in her finery at some royal court."

"Not a ball," said Amy.

"Perhaps, perhaps." Rob spread his hand. "At times, the prince has been bewitched to forget his princess, and she has to attend a ball to rouse his memory."

"Finery," said Rosaleen. "I will have to appear at his father's court."

#

Outside was a shock, past the sight of the garden. Even the growth of trees. She had guessed that she had not slept a week or two, then, or a few months, but this brought it to bear.

Then she looked down into the village. It took a few minutes, watching people walking about.

"I didn't think I would *need* the horn, not *here*! Not yet!"

"Don't blow it yet," said Adam. "We must have knowledge, and there are, after all, no soldiers visible."

And precious few men. Rosaleen breathed in and out with care. The houses had not been burnt, and they had not been rebuilt either.

They had climbed down half the path before anyone noticed them. Then a woman dropped her basket and turned as pale as if she had seen a ghost rising, still dripping, from the lake where he had drowned.

A minute later, Rosaleen realized that it was Polly. A child clung at her skirts. Perhaps another one in the cradle. . . . Rosaleen forced her breath in and out. The child was not so old as Polly had been when Rosaleen had first met her.

Though not much younger, said another thought.

Before she gathered her wits, Tom hailed Polly and asked for news.

"Be grateful you slept, Your Highness," said Polly, sounding hoarse, and with many glances at Rosaleen. "We think most of the men hid well enough in the woods, but they can't come out again to tell us they are well."

She wasn't dressed in black, Rosaleen told herself, and then remembered that Polly could be out of mourning.

"Your Majesty."

Rosaleen blinked at the dark young man, with a limp, who walked up.

"Not Your Highness. Your Majesty." He turned from Polly to Rosaleen and bowed. "My kin sent me here after the army lamed me. But if the army knew you were here, they would come to fetch you."

She felt curiously cold. She did not know them, but—"Because my father and brothers are dead."

He bowed again. "Your lady mother as well, too, I fear."

For a moment, Rosaleen stood in silence, her thoughts going this way and that. Her people, her kingdom. Still—

"I must go and fetch my bridegroom, so that the curse is broken. I can not serve as queen before that."

She hesitated, but she knew what she had to say. "I would have to refuse if soldiers came for me." The horn hung heavy in its bag. She had thought only of fighting foreigners. She might yet have to win her kingdom back—she scarcely dared to leave it in King Henry's hands—but not yet. "Best for me to leave in secret and return with my prince's aid to restore the land."

"Very much so," he said.

Polly nodded.

"First," said Ned, "we should prepare ourselves for the road. And visit the church to pray for the dead, and to commend ourselves to God, because this will be a hard journey."

The villagers talked, of course, as they bought food and clothes and a few other things that they could find in the village. Less than before she had slept. They had grown poor. Rosaleen thought that some hid in their cellars for fear she would ask for what they could not spare. They could not use the coin to buy from other villages what the others did not have either.

Find your prince, she told herself. Or your attempts to help them will founder.

She ignored when someone said that Maid Maleen had not returned to rescue her father's kingdom after the war, and told herself she could not see who said it.

A few peasants remembered seeing a young man head toward the castle, and leave again, though they were uncertain. Might have been some kind of woodcutter or forester, and perhaps not so young. Someone who went by the castle. A month before.

"Or maybe it was two," said old Dobbin. He scowled. "Three?"

From the chatter, they would never determine the day. Rosaleen bit back a sigh. A princess must act in a seemly manner always. A queen even more so. She would not have Lady Gilliane ashamed of her. And it did not matter, she supposed. They did agree he came from the south, which would let her chase after him with unseemly haste.

Whenever she came upon little children, they stopped to stare. Other children ran up to stare, one or two sitting down abruptly on the dirt as soon as they saw her. Once, she came about a corner to see other children, a little older, played at a prince saving a princess from an ogre. She thought she recognized the tale, but it would be oafish to stand and stare. And set the little children a bad example. Their mothers, when they caught them staring, tried to hustle them away, talking of manners.

She and her companions went on, to the church. There villagers joined them in prayer. Rosaleen looked up at the crucifix and felt coldly aware that the journey would be longer than any other she had gone on. Even the journey she had taken to come here, as a child, when she was too small to remember it at all. Certainly every journey she had been on since.

Sunlight shining through the windows, making the stained glass as colorful as jewels, began to dim.

She stood. Night approached.

The villagers rose and gathered about her, wishing her well, calling for St. Bernard and St. Christopher to pray for her, invoking Heaven's blessing on her.

She wished them well, called for St. Bernard to pray for them, and Heaven to bless them, and felt cold. She might see them again in the morning, as they would rise as early to work as she would to journey. But perhaps not. They would be about their labors, and she could not dally.

Before she went to bed, she put the handkerchief in a bag, to fit to her belt, under her skirt. She did not want to lose it if she had pull the horn out in haste.

And she might need the horn in haste.

#

The morning was very, very gray. Rosaleen pulled her cloak about her against the droplets as they inched down the trail damp with dew, past the village utterly veiled in fog. The castle was gone in the gray, and the forest as well.

When they passed the last house, most of the village was gone from sight as well.

Rosaleen bit her lip and mentioned the danger of deserters.

"What, you do not think they all struck a deal with a devil?" said Ellen. "And are off gadding about until the deal comes due, and the devil asks the riddle?"

"He could have asked it by now," said Rosaleen. "And they could have gotten his grandmother to tell them the answer. It has been some years."

In the silence, as trees loomed out of the mists, Adam said, "Would depend on how many years he gave them."

"Then," said Tom, "we'll have to face them when they appear." He peered up at her. "Are you carrying a message that orders the death of the bearer?"

"No," said Rosaleen. "It wouldn't be from someone who could order the marriage of a prince, either. I shall just have to win him without the bandits altering such a message."

"First step," said Amy, "is to find him, and the first step to that is to get out of the mountains."

Ellen harumphed. "Are we trusting the peasant for the right direction?"

For a moment they were all silent. The air was still, without a whisper of breeze. Rosaleen could hear water dripping from trees.

"It's as good a direction as we are likely to get," said Rob. "Ask along the way, and if we do not find him, we must look for a little old woman in the woods."

To get directions, and yet Ned winked broadly to the others. Perhaps he thought she could not see him, out of the corner of her eye. Then, if she did not trust them, she would have been wiser to steal off in the night.

"Ah, such wonderful company," caroled Tom. "No one crabby at being roused in the morning!"

"Watch your step, Tom," said Adam. "Ground's slippery. And we don't want to lug you about because you broke your leg."

Tom eyed him.

Rosaleen laughed. And watched her step. The rocks were indeed slippery.

#

These roads had never been crowded, but were so empty now that Rosaleen hesitated whenever they saw another traveler, even an old woman lugging firewood to her hut.

The day they saw a company of rough-clad men, the dwarfs hustled her aside before she saw any more of them.

She crouched with them among brambles and heard the rough-voiced complaints from the way. The deserters had seen them, but they were gone so thoroughly that some of the deserters doubted their eyes.

Rosaleen looked back and forth from dwarf to dwarf within the bramble. And would have said nothing even without the peril of being overheard.

Her fingers drifted toward the horn, and she swallowed. She did not draw it out, but she did not take her hand away as the men quarreled about where to go next.

A long time after the voices had vanished with distance, they walked from the brambles. Rosaleen moved slowly with stiffness. The dwarfs grumbled about how the brambles caught. They staggered out onto the way, and walked onward.

"Briskly now," said Ned. "They lost us time."

Briskly though they went, that evening, no village or inn hove into view. Ned pointed out a hut in the woods, and it was a poor, chilly thing, with the stars visible, but there they slept.

In the next village, by a river, they heard talk of how desperate the men had been, and that they had killed Robin Jackson before they died.

None of the men with boats were willing to be hired to bear them downstream. They crossed the bridge and went on, afoot.

#

Back in the mountains, she could still see the snow, but on the road, it felt so hot that Rosaleen doubted that there would ever be snow to melt. She wondered how long this journey could take, and told herself that crossing thrice ten kingdoms might still lie ahead of her.

They trudged through the dust and, one day, came to a crossroads without a sign. Or a stone warning that one way meant hunger and thirst, another that their horses would live, and they would die, and the third that their horses would die, and they would live.

Perhaps, thought Rosaleen crossly, because they had no horses. Or perhaps because any way they went, they would die of heat and thirst.

Molly thoughtfully took out a bottle and offered it to her. Rosaleen drank the spring water. Far from cold, of course. She wished there was a boulder to sit on. It was so hot.

"I shall get more water," said Ned. "You can rest in the shade while I go to the spring." He collected the bottles swiftly, and headed off into the woods.

Rosaleen walked into the deeper shade of a tree back along the path. She sighed, and said, "I hope the prince is like the one Tattercoats married."

Ellen arched an eyebrow. Amy, not quite frowning in thought, turned toward her.

"If I had to go to the ball dressed like this, all the lords and ladies would laugh. But Tattercoats met her prince on the road, and he did not care that she was dressed in tatters."

"She did have a gooseherd playing a pipe to dance to," said Molly solemnly.

"And he vanished afterward. Still, her prince did not care that the music was magical."

"We did bring gowns," said Molly, even more solemnly. "And fine ones."

If she had time to dress before she met the prince, that would help. Or perhaps found a place to dress and meet him again after they met. She sighed. She did not want a prince who threw a comb or the wash water after the maidservant who was secretly the princess whom he had fallen in love with at the ball.

Though that prince would still be better than blowing the horn and having the prince take her seriously because his city overflowed with soldiers. She could hope it was needed only for the king. Better yet, not at all.

She frowned. The fairy had definitely said that a prince would kiss her and wake her, and they would marry happily, but when the other fairy said that the prince would leave, and she would have to find him, it might mean he had ascended to the throne between the kiss and now.

On the other hand, the fairy had promised a happy marriage, and the fairy of Pine Tree Falls was famed for her skill with that.

Rosaleen let her breath. The heat made her thoughts all muzzy.

"Good news!" Ned waved a bottle. "I was not the only one at the spring! We should head toward the right-hand road!"

#

Ned fell back toward her, and Amy watched him come. She thought Rosaleen had not noticed how he picked them out one by one, to speak in a low voice.

"The Dwarf of Coldwater Springs sends his greetings."

"I trust he sent enough clear water for her to drink," said Ellen. "This is far longer than her journey to get the horn, and she is not used to the heat."

"No," said Ned, "but he told me where to find more."

"I suppose that will do," said Amy. "I doubt he could send enough water for us all. It's hot for us, too. And a long journey. Easier if only we could use magic."

They looked at Rosaleen, ahead.

"Be courageous, and steadfast," said Ned. "The fairy meant it for a curse. We can foil it."

"The prince," said Molly sourly, "could have helped. Left something with his name. Or even left his dagger and took her locket. Anything to help."

Sunlight splattered the road through gaps in the leaves, and the air was so still that the light did not move as they trudged on.

"We'll get there," said Amy. "Somehow."

Molly hoped it would not take too long. The leaves, even this far south, were beginning to turn gold and red. At least in the swamps, where it always started.

Wouldn't end there, she thought, and looked at where the road curved ahead.

#

About the bend, the forest opened into fields newly harvested. And pasture, with small stands of trees here and there. Rivers with boats on them, and roads with laden carts. Indeed, she could make out a fair sized town ahead.

"A kingdom!" said Rosaleen in delight. The dwarfs scrambled to catch up and exclaim over how lovely it was, after the weeks in the forest.

The pastures were colorful with flowers, and clouds dotted the skies. Not enough to replace the shade the trees had given. Then, the breezes were more frequent.

You don't even know whether this is *his* kingdom, Rosaleen chided herself. You might still have cross thrice ten kingdoms to find him. You might even have go to the East Wind, the West Wind, the South Wind, and the North Wind, and only the North Wind has heard of him. It was, after all, a curse that he would be hard for you to find.

She could not quell her mood.

#

They would have stopped at the inn no matter what happened, as the sky turned orange, for the beds and shelter, and the cook. Still, Tom talked with the stable boys before they even spoke to the inn-keeper. It proved unneeded. The inn was rife with talk of the ill king and his three sons' quest, and Rosaleen's heart hammered as she tried to listen to everything at once.

One henwife talked of the youngest having poisoned the king.

"Don't you know," said one young man, a farmer on the road, "that whenever that happens, the older sons maligned the youngest?"

She tossed her head, and pocketed the coins from her eggs. "Whenever that happens, the kingdom believes the older sons until something happens to prove him guiltless. So—" Her finger jabbed out toward the man. "I'm just following my part in the tale." She put her hands on her hips. "If it is a tale."

"What happened to the youngest?" said Molly, with perfect mildness. "Sent out into the forest to be executed?"

"As usual?" said Amy.

Rosaleen could not fathom how calmly they could speak. Adam already bargained for a room and talked of how many travelers the inn could expect while she—her sprouting hope was overshadowed by new fear. Finding the kingdom was not enough. She needed to find the prince. If he had fled his father's lands in fear for his life, she might have to find the four winds to track him down.

Adam cheerily led the way up the stairs, with Molly and Amy following as the other went to fetch the meal, and she joined them, and bit her lip.

Find the four winds to track the prince down—assuming the Fairy of Pine Tree Falls had actually worked her spell, and the other fairy had not broken it. And so, worse, he might find work as a gardener's boy in another kingdom, and save it from an invading army, and win the princess of that land. Thus leaving her trapped with a curse that could never, ever break.

She shivered for all the heat. Perhaps they would actually execute him. A reed might grow on his grave, so that a pipe made from it would announce the truth, but that would not save him.

They closed the door behind themselves, and she said, "We need all the tales we can get, to learn what to do."

"They will all glean every bit of news they can before they bring up the meal," Amy assured her.

That gave her little encouragement. The sky turned deep crimson and violet, the other dwarfs came up the stairs, bearing their dinner, telling how Ned stayed below to listen to one more account, and Tom informed them all that the youngest prince was the one who had come to her castle.

"His name is Liam," said Tom.

Rosaleen nodded slowly. Her heart was beating not faster, but harder.

"Some old women wept speaking of him," said Molly. "Not all believe his brothers' tale."

"Huh," said Tom. He waved his hand. "Older brothers."

"We must go to the castle," said Rosaleen. They all looked at her. "Perhaps the youngest was thrown into prison, or the like. But I must show up his brothers' claims, and then—" She waved a hand with bread in it. "Where could I better find where the prince might have gone? That someone saw him going south did not go ill for us."

Heads bobbed in agreement, all about the table.

"I do not recommend feigning to get to the castle," said Amy briskly. "A troupe of actors could get in, yes, but you have that handkerchief that Lady Gilliane gave you. Unless you arrive as a princess, you will not be able to insist." She frowned. "Or rather, a queen."

Ned charged up the stairs, his footsteps ringing before his arrival. Panting, he stood in the doorway. "King Stefan's guard. They are here. Asking about, and for, the company of strangers asking about the princes."

A moment's silence, then Tom said, "We want to stick together. They will separate us."

Some decisions were easy. Rosaleen took out the horn. For a moment, she contemplated it and the still unanswered question of whether the soldiers could be sent back. Then she heard footsteps on the stairs, heavier than Ned's, and more numerous.

Molly pointed to the window.

True enough, the sound would be deafening. She opened the window to the chill evening breeze and the evening star gleaming over the last, darkest red of sunset. Only the light from the inn let her see the people below, the guards or those gawking at them.

She put the horn to her mouth and blew it. The note rang out, people gawked from the streets, and shouts came from below. In the room, a soldier appeared, facing the door, and drew his sword. The dwarfs pulled back.

Rosaleen heard the footsteps, and judged. One soldier was not enough to face that company. She blew the horn again, and the king's guards opened the door to face a dozen soldiers, led by the first one.

She lowered the horn. When the guards did not move forward, she glanced at the soldiers. The first one who appeared wore the uniform of a captain. She could not remember whether he had worn it when he first appeared.

"What is your business here with our lady?" said her captain.

The other captain's gaze shifted over to Rosaleen. He bowed.

"My lady. His Majesty the King would wish so great a lady to be escorted with all courtesy, and also that he might know what such a lady wished in his kingdom."

Rosaleen nodded as regally as she could manage in her traveling clothes. "I have indeed come to see your king. Your men will escort me to court in the morning."

The captain bowed again. "I will send word ahead this night, of your coming—my lady?" He raised his head a bit and lifted an eyebrow. "My Lady Incognita?"

Amy cleared her throat to announce her. As queen. Rosaleen, still feeling like a princess, felt glad that she should leave such things to her attendants.

#

She woke before the sky was lighter than charcoal gray, and the dwarfs already bustled about the room. Soldiers stood on guard at the door—inside and out. Ellen produced a gown, and she dressed and saw as the light increased that it was one of her better gowns. Not good enough for court unless she overtly intended to arrive travel-stained, but finer than the gown she had worn the other day.

She took care to put the handkerchief in it.

The sky was still gray when they descended the stairs, Rosaleen and the dwarfs carefully surrounded by soldiers. King Stefan's guard already stood ready to escort them.

Her captain said, his voice low, "He had sent for more soldiers."

Rosaleen drew a deep breath to steady herself. "Will you see them come quickly enough? I do not want to summon more myself until needed, it will break the peace."

Her captain nodded, sharply, and asked no more questions. They walked.

It did not take long before it was clear that traveling as a commoner had its advantages. King Stefan's guards kept her from being bothered by people, but they attracted a crowd that no effort could keep from slowing the journey. Indeed, some of the crowd were making an effort to slow them, to make it easier to gawk at the soldiers in their strange uniforms, this queen in her almost plain gown, and her sole attendants being dwarfs.

They heard more talk along the way, of how ill King Stefan had been, how much worse his youngest had made him, and how grateful he was to his two elder sons.

"Thinking he could just be the youngest, and thus claim the throne!" said one old woman. "The little fool!"

A girl asked whether this—queen had anything to do with that, and the king's guard forced the way through this knot.

Rosaleen walked along, said nothing, avoided the mud puddles on the way—there weren't many—and felt keenly aware of the handkerchief, secure in her pocket and ready to overturn all their tales.

At least, the dwarfs had brought finery, so that she sparkled enough to appear a princess—a queen—and demand audience, even with a king.

A shout resounded ahead. Followed by a long tirade, unintelligible with distance, but furious. King Stefan's guard shifted and squared up around her, and she peered ahead. A crowd on the bridge looked sullen and moved slowly. Some of them were as angry about those standing about as the guards were.

Rosaleen let her breath out. Perhaps summoning more soldiers would be wiser and quicker, enough to dispense with the sparkle.

It ill befit a queen to not try courtesy first, Rosaleen told herself. She should not shame Lady Gilliane's memory by forgetting her lessons.

The bridge cleared enough for them to pass, and someone cheered the princess from far-away, and many others joined in, joyfully. Rosaleen had to fight the blush. Being queen would mean many crowds and many cheers. She waved at the crowd, smiled at the children, and heard the cheers redouble.

And indeed, over the next three days, other crowds sometimes cheered her.

The dawn of the fourth day—a delicate pink and cream dawn—her captain pointed out the castle to her, far off in the distance. Her heart sank. It had be much closer than what she had already traveled, she told herself, but that did not rouse her spirits.

Molly came up beside her. "When should we change your clothes? Travel stained is no way to present yourself at court, but better travel-stained finery than to look common."

"Tell the soldiers to have a tent ready, to put up at the gates."

#

The castle was immense. It loomed over the city like a mountain over the forest.

Rosaleen tried to act as if she had seen such things before, though she had left her father's castle before she could remember whether it was smaller or larger or the same size as this.

As they came under the city gates, the walls hid the castle from sight. Instead, the castle walls loomed.

Putting up the tent and putting on her finery did not help. She felt as if she had dressed up with all the peasant girls while they played out their fairy tales, and now had to appear before King Stefan dressed like that.

She straightened and let her guards escort her. A queen must not cringe.

The streets thronged. Some people still tried to go about their duties without paying heed, but they were few compared to those who gawked, or grumbled, or cheered. Quite a few places had banners flying from windows. And despite the crowds, their path was more clear than it had been on the road. The castle gates stood before them within an hour.

She swept on.

The throne room, hung with scarlet banners, thronged with courtiers, all glittering, but a path lay open between the door and the golden throne. A white-haired and bearded man sat, crowned, dressed in scarlet, and looking perfectly hale. Two young men stood to either hand. One, she noted, growing a bit thick in the midsection, but both wore finery in red, second only to King Stefan's.

She stood within the door. Far enough in that her soldiers could escort her.

Her captain announced her purpose briefly enough, and King Stefan nodded.

"My son Kevin brought back a golden apple to heal me. It must have come from your castle's garden."

The princes showed no reaction. The one growing plump looked almost fatuous. If they intended to brazen it out—Rosaleen drew out the handkerchief and threw it on the carpet before herself.

"Let him say so himself, and then walk over this handkerchief."

Silence lasted after that. She fought against blinking, and looked from prince to prince.

Don't bite your lip, she told herself. You will find your prince.

The fatter prince's face contorted. The other one looked straight ahead, as if he had been asked to juggle for the court, or perhaps to wallow in mud, and wished to spare her the indignity of taking her at her word.

"Kevin, you are the elder. You must go first," said King Stefan.

"At the behest of this—woman?" said Kevin, with his lip curled. "Let us have no nonsense. Any woman can claim to be a queen, and we already know this one to be a witch, conjuring up things. Do you wish to be the king who remarried after promising his first wife that he would marry only a princess accustomed to living in great courts, so her position would not go to her head? And who then broke his promise because the witch claimed to have been exiled from her court? She was a misery to her stepsons thereafter."

"You who searched for days and weeks and months to find that golden apple that healed me can also walk over a handkerchief," said King Stefan, neither mild nor fierce, but stern and regal.

Rosaleen kept her face as steady as a mask. She could not rescind her demand now. Not though she knew the answer already.

Some aged courtier started to murmur soothingly, unctuously, that it was only a handkerchief, such as anyone might tread on any day at court by mischance. What could it do?

"Huh," said the other. "It's only a piece of cloth."

"Then walk over it, Ewan," said Kevin.

"At the command of some crow in borrowed feathers, coming in force to our lands?"

The captain drew up beside her, his hand on his sword. The other soldiers shifted about her. Her hand twitched. She might not need the horn, even if the prince were not warned by this.

"Walk over it," said King Stefan, almost mildly.

His face was implacable, and showed no surprise. Ewan flinched. Slowly he walked up, glancing at her, and stepped over the handkerchief.

He fell flat on his face, and screamed in agony.

Rosaleen felt queasy, but King Stefan did not look surprised. Her own soldiers stood like statues, and she tried to imitate them. Molly thoughtfully picked up the handkerchief before standing like the rest of the dwarfs. Courtiers milled about uselessly and exclaimed and sometimes slipped off, but servants, heedless of both their own king and of Rosaleen, hurried forward to help. Though pale and shaking, they ignored the wild blows the prince sent their way, and had his broken leg bound up and himself drugged on poppy extract before anyone noticed that Kevin had vanished.

Servants bore off Ewan through a side door as courtiers exclaimed and looked about and demanded explanations of their own servants. The king's guards hurried about, looking, as King Stefan looked older with each moment that passed.

In that commotion, King Stefan closed his eyes for a minute before raising his voice. "Liam showed as much judgment. More, indeed, than I did. I was too angry to think before I spoke. He fled before he faced danger."

Shortly thereafter that a page boy returned with news that Prince Kevin had fled. His horse had been ready.

"As if he knew that he would need to flee," said Rosaleen.

"Send word to the ports," said King Stefan. "I wish to have news of his departure."

But, thought Rosaleen, she had not found her prince.

#

Rosaleen stared out the window. Trees covered the hills before her.

Behind her, King Stefan and his huntsmen spoke. The huntsmen were as chary of speech as if the king had ordered Liam's death, and speaking of his life was an admission that they had defied him.

Nevertheless, they admitted, in due course, that they had set the prince on a path, to the north. To the wilderness, the forest and the mountains, that she and the dwarfs had walked around on the way south.

She turned about. "I do not know how far you can guide me, but we should leave as soon as possible. Summer is passing. I remember the mountain snows."

After a minute of silence, one huntsman bowed. "As you wish, Your Majesty. We leave at dawn tomorrow. If it pleases you."

She nodded, and the company slowly dissolved.

"This way, Your Majesty," murmured Molly. In the corridor, she said, "Ready at dawn, then, Your Majesty."

"Of course," said Rosaleen. Then, a bit acid, "Perhaps we need to impress on the huntsman our willingness to journey, but I thought you knew mine."

"We sometimes failed of dawn itself," said Molly. "This time, that will not do. And winter is none so far away. We need haste."

"Also," said Tom, "dawn gets later by the day."

#

Mists coiled about the courtyard. The torchlight did not reach far.

No one talked of ethereal white maidens who lured the traveler off cliffs. At least, thought Rosaleen, not where she could hear them. Then, the dwarfs knew she knew, the huntsmen still eyed her warily as the foreign princess—queen, and her own soldiers might not know of the tales.

Tom's voice came from the mist ahead as he cheerfully reminded the huntsman that he and several of his fellows were dwarfs.

"Nothing like a good mountain range for a dwarf, we have no excuse!"

"Never let the dwarfs of the mountains hear you talk like that," said the huntsman.

"Suits me," said Tom. "Better to be off and doing rather than standing about gabbing. The question is whether everyone else is ready to be off."

Rosaleen rolled her eyes, glad that the gloom and mist would hide it, but unable to suppress so unprincessly an act. Or even unqueenly.

The soldiers started crisply off. Rosaleen fell quietly into her place in the company.

They traveled out the gates of the city, and a fair distance on the road, before the mists melted off, and revealed the blue of the mountains ahead.

Part VI

We can't go into the mountains forever, thought Rosaleen, walking about against stiffness. One day, we would get up and start to go out of the mountains. She looked up at the peaks. It would not be today. The heights were rosy with dawn, and their slopes covered in shadows. The mountains grew still higher before them, though the foresters still knew the passes.

She should trust Heaven and go to eat her breakfast.

"I have it!" Adam burst out from beneath the trees. "I have the way we must go! Make haste, make haste, we need not sleep under the stars today!"

Rosaleen hesitated, and then ran over and ate in haste. Hope stirred, and she realized she had not truly thought they could arrive.

#

Rosaleen looked at the slope before her. No trail. If the trees did not have knotted roots sprawling over the earth, she could not have climbed it. With them, despite the way they straggled, and how they seemed to never leave a stride of the ground uncovered, she still felt uncertain.

And Adam called this a way. She looked up the towering trees, their branches high overhead all but blocking the sunlight, and she wondered if there were no other way.

"Your Majesty," said a soldier, offering his arm. He steadied her when she staggered, and once she steadied him. She reached a flat part of the slope, and caught her breath, feeling a little envious of the dwarfs' nimble feet.

"Over here!" Adam's voice boomed so loudly it echoed, and Rosaleen, for a moment, did not want to move. But she inched her way along the ridge, past stands of ferns, and walked through a thicket of brambles where no amount of pulling back branches prevented being prodded and pricked with thorns as she worked her way out.

And onto a road.

A rather well made road, though either side was thick with brambles. Trees towered over them, but they had, she thought, come through the thinnest place in the hedge. Their only choice was the road. As if—she smoothed out her skirt—such a guide were not the most welcome thing they could have found beside the prince she sought. Adam already talked with a traveler, who talked of the city just ahead. A vague term on the road, but still, a direction.

When, within an hour, the city walls appeared ahead, she could have wept with relief. Guards in uniforms of silver and drab brown already stood at the gate, as if they expected her. They heard her purpose, to see their king—or lord—and conferred among themselves. She stood for a minute on the way, wondering whether her words had been wise—but no one could bring soldiers into a kingdom without the king's hearing of it.

A dozen guards formed up, and another told her captain that they would escort her, and her company, to the castle. Within moments, they brought her down streets with all their half-timbered houses. People glanced and murmured as in King Stefan's city, but they did not clump in the way.

The castle appeared, now and again, when the streets allowed the sight, and then, abruptly, it loomed up before her. She swallowed. Smaller than King Stefan's, but much larger than the hunting lodge. With new guards at the castle gates, openly looking for them.

One stepped forward. "He will see her in the small chamber, beside the garden."

A pert little page boy, red-haired, came forward to bow. "This way, Your Majesty."

The path led, briefly, through the garden. A lean young man straightened from the flowers he worked on. He started, stared, and, blushing, turned back to the flowers. A breeze sent a cascade of golden leaves onto him, over his blond hair. (Not true gold, said an impish thought.)

Rosaleen looked ahead. The king first, she told herself, courtesy requires it, but she could not keep her heart from hammering. All the more when she remembered that Prince Liam would have seen her, and then she could feel the heat in her face.

The doorway to the chamber stood open to the garden. The floor bore a carpet of blue and green, intricately worked, and a bear sat in the middle of it, with fur of chestnut red, and watching her with sagacious eyes.

Rosaleen gulped. He could make a meal of her in two bites, and Lady Gilliane had not included this kingdom in lessons.

"I mean no discourtesy to you, sir, but though my teacher endeavored to instruct me in all nearby kingdoms, yet she had not heard of this one, and I know nothing of it."

The bear nodded. "You may continue to call me sir, madame."

The title made her feel older than she was. More than learning that she was queen had.

"I have come to your country because of a fairy's christening gift. I have reason to believe that the prince I am to marry lives in your kingdom."

"He does," said the bear, grandly.

Rosaleen blinked. That was pat. She had come here, she had found the prince. Her tongue touched her lips. Then, she had not met him yet.

Moments later, a guard appeared by the doorway, and the gardener, the golden-haired young man, stood by him.

You are a queen, Rosaleen told herself, staring at the young man and trying not to. A clearer look at him—as he took a clearer look at her.

He bowed, deeply, with elegance. "I must beg your pardon, madame. I was the one who intruded into your castle, and your garden." He colored again, more furiously, as he straightened. "And your bed-chamber. I meant only to take an apple—"

"There was a curse," said Rosaleen. He fell silent. "A curse that meant that you had to leave before it could break because of your arrival." She smiled. "You did break it."

He blinked.

"But first." She produced the handkerchief, and told what was needed. She felt no surprise when he walked over it without difficulty. Indeed, with less difficulty than she found in marshaling the words to tell him about her christening, and the curse of the last fairy on her. He blushed again when he told her how he had tried to wake her.

"I hope," said Rosaleen, "that you are not too affronted that the fairy had thus arranged your life."

He smiled, and it lit up his face. "Heaven bless the fairy for her good deeds for you. And what they mean for me."

Then they were silent, and she was turning furiously red, she could feel the heat in her face, and she knew that she did not blush beautifully.

The bear chortled. "I trust you are not seeking to return home, Your Majesty."

Rosaleen started.

"As the last survivor of your family's house, you must not risk the winter storms, even to spare your kingdom the war." He waved a paw and looked between them. "Your company can easily stay the winter. You need not pour out your hearts all at once."

Liam bowed and said something about the garden.

"Then let us go into the garden," said Rosaleen. He looked at her, and she must have been as red as a rose, not only on her cheeks, but to her ears. "I did not live in my father's castle within my memory.

At—that castle—you saw me at—I would sit in the garden and talk with the gardeners. Sometimes I would even help."

The bear chortled again. "Let her give advice on the garden, if she pleases. To make it as lovely as other kingdom's."

#

The bear ordered a servant to make them welcome while Rosaleen went into the garden, and the man showed the seven of them to a room. Ned looked about with approval. It was large and well furnished, and better yet had seats before the windows, letting them look down into the garden.

"The fairest flowers being those two," said Tom.

"It's a good thing we did not offer to help with the garden," said Ned. The prince, Liam if he heard right, continued with this work. Putting the mulch carefully in place and not slapping it about, which showed prudence and judgment. Then, the spell did say that they would live happily ever after.

"Is this," said Molly, "one of those tales where the princess doesn't go back? Will Rosaleen play Maid Maleen, and abandon the kingdom?"

Adam waved his hand. "Maid Maleen's kingdom had been ruined, everyone driven off. Rosaleen needs to go back for her subjects' sake. Also, she has an army, if she wants one."

"She may be wary of that," said Ellen.

"She knows her duty," said Amy. "Lady Gilliane got that part of her education right. If anything, she may spend too much effort on saving the kingdom."

"Of course she won't," said Ned. "Not if it will make her, or her prince, unhappy."

"Besides, her subjects will be glad of a queen," said Rob.

"She'll have time to reflect," said the bear, heartily, from the doorway. "Winter comes too swiftly for her to make it to her kingdom, or even his, before the snows will trap her." It lumbered in. "She can sit and decorate her wedding gown with embroidery while they talk."

Adam looked at the bear with narrowed eyes. "Isn't that early? One might suspect that a person might have had a hand with it."

The bear sat on the rug. "Even if I could do such weather work, I did not know when she could come. I might have sent storms that would have kept her out, or killed her. No, if there's witchery afoot, perhaps you should look back to the days of the christening. To keep them the winter long in this refuge might help with the working out of her spell."

Ned sat back, thinking.

"You could have worked since she came," said Ellen.

"I could have?" After a moment, the bear added, "I would have to work such spells at all to know whether it could be done in so short a time."

Ned laughed out loud. "You will have to show that he can work such magic to prove your cases."

"Hush, all of you," said Tom. "Come and watch the two of them in the garden."

Adam glared.

"Do be reasonable," said Rob. "They must deal with his father, and the armies in her kingdom. They may be glad of the snowstorms for the respite they grant."

"How very true," said Tom.

Rob scowled. "No, we'll get the huntsmen to talk with him. King Stefan will not be a problem, and the huntsmen can even persuade Prince Liam that it is so."

"Especially given that there will be time to persuade him," said Ned. "What time they can spare from their wooing."

"They will value the time," said Molly.

"They will value the peace more after they reconcile with his father, and win back her kingdom," said Adam, his voice hollow.

"They," said the bear, " might have been happier if there had been no spell. But there was. They might have been happier if they could leave the mountains within days of arrival. But they can't." He waved a paw in the air. "You managed with the spell. You will manage with the winter."

In the silence after, peals of Rosaleen's laughter came up from the garden.

"Will Liam recognize any of you?" said the bear.

"No," said Adam. "Neither would either of his brothers, even if they could tell one dwarf from another." Ned snorted. "We had friends who actually spoke with the princes."

Part VII

Against the wall, by gray daylight and candlelight, Molly, Amy, and Ellen were all hard at work at sewing. The plain work, an impending wedding did not mean nothing else was needed, but they were stitching so hard that Rosaleen did not think they would hear any words by the hearth, which was ablaze.

Liam leaned forward as if he could spy out dragons in the ruby-red coals.

By the doorway, Rosaleen stood, feeling foolish.

She felt certain she had not made a peep, but he looked over and stood.

"Watching the weather?" he said.

"It worries me," she said. "I lived in the mountains."

He came over, offered her his arm, and brought her over, by the window. The view was imperfect, but she could see that the guards were changing. Torchlight spread out the scene, tinging it with orange.

It snowed. Enormous, light, fluffy snowflakes. As far as she could see by torchlight, snow fell. Already, the garden lay covered. The taller bushes had snow clumped on their higher branches, but their trunks were engulfed by whiteness, and the smaller bushes were among the higher clumps of snow. Clouds muffled the stars, and when the wind blew, more snow drifted toward the castle, as well as away. Rosaleen smiled.

"A blanket of snow, all over the mountains," she said to Liam.

"I wouldn't want to lie under that blanket," he said, dryly

"It has its virtues, I saw them while living in the mountains. The winters with a drought left the gardens and orchards and forests all bare. It was deadly. This will preserve all your handiwork better, over the winter." She tilted her head to one side. "Did you often lose plants in the garden, over winter? Or was it mild enough that they need no protection?"

"It was the dryness, usually, that killed them," admitted Liam. "Mulching would save most of them, but sometimes, even then, dryness would kill."

Rosaleen nodded, and her tongue felt heavy in her mouth. She should suggest they go by the fire, where it was warmer, but could not speak.

Liam glanced at her, and she felt her face heat.

"It is just as well that the bear shows every sign of being a perfect host," said Liam.

Rosaleen felt her face grow hotter. "And just as well that the roses are past blooming. Even such a paragon should not be tested so far as to steal one of his roses."

Liam raised an eyebrow.

"On top of its being theft, of course," said Rosaleen. "But the peasant lads sometimes took roses from the garden for their lassies. The gardeners only grumbled."

#

The snow melted easily and quickly. Within a week, the garden was a morass of mud and sticks and dead flowers. The streets outside had rivulets in them.

"I think," said Rosaleen, with grave majesty, to the dwarfs and the captain of her guard, "that it would be as bad to fare forth in that mud as in the snow."

The captain bowed and said, "There is much reason to think that it will snow again, and soon. These mountains has never known a winter where snow storm did not follow snow storm."

Dark gray clouds billowed on the horizon.

"How very true," said Rosaleen. She gathered her skirts to keep them out of the mud and went back in.

Ned glanced about. Neither the captain nor the other dwarfs so much as looked at the door, though the air was raw. True, none of them knew where the prince was. Awkward to have to avoid two young lovers, and all the more when they were royal.

"At least she did not need soothing," said the captain.

"She is used to such matters," said Molly.

"Unfortunately," said Ned, "if she is frustrated and thinks the matter of importance enough, she will go alone."

"She was only a child then," said Adam. "She has grown in prudence."

#

A woman came to the door, with a small child. She looked old. Then, beggary could age the young, next to the prosperous.

Rosaleen started to reckon her purse. Then a kitchen maid came out to speak to the beggar, and her breath came out.

Liam came up beside her.

He looked for a moment as if he wrestled with what to say. Then, finally, "The bear was kind to me as a poor beggar lad."

Rosaleen blinked. She had not thought of that. "There must be many such unfortunates in my kingdom," she said. "The battles have ravaged it. Are still ravaging it, and will ravage it until my return and even past it. Especially the prosperous lands."

More snow drifted down on the scene outside. Just a few flakes, enough to make it unwise to take to the road.

"I trust that if, in due course, we have a child, and I give that child a coin to give a beggar woman with her child, you will not complain that the beggars' brats get along?"

Rosaleen laughed. "My governess made certain I heard all those tales. I will imagine no such thing. And I think you must reconcile with your father before that day."

The kitchen maid ushered the beggars both inside.

Rosaleen sighed a little. It was cold by the window, and though she could not smell any smoke, the warmth within was testimony enough to the fire. She turned from the window.

The fire danced a bit over the logs, sending up plumes of sparks now and again, but mostly it slumbered as deep red coals, warming the room. Such a lovely warmth. She glanced sideways at Liam.

"We should tell stories by the fire," she said.

A tray of pastries sat by the fireplace. Strawberry filling, and nicely crispy. She looked at them for a moment, considering who was match making.

Perhaps all the castle was. She cast a sideways glance at the bride-groom.

#

The bear talked with woodsmen about the state of the roads—muddy and with fords that were impassable—and how, nevertheless, Rosaleen and Liam should be ready to leave the moment the way was clear.

She barely managed to keep her answers coherent at meals. Waiting was making her giddy.

Rosaleen danced about her chamber, and wished the gown were not done, but it did hang in her wardrobe, safe from all eyes, and another stitch of embroidery would ruin the pattern.

She went to the window, breathed in the balmy air, and looked down. The apple trees were pink: palely with opened blossoms, and jewel-dark where the buds were furled.

The sun glinted on Liam's hair. She scurried toward the stairs. They had only fleeting moments before it would be improper for them to speak together, before she withdrew from all company except her servants' until the wedding. She would not eat dinner with him and the bear that night.

Liam was at the door before she reached it. He bowed and offered her his arm, and they walked through the garden, among the blossoming apple trees, talking idly, of this and that.

A mossy statue appeared before them. Not of man or beast.

Liam nodded at the sight of it. "Our garden had a statue of that old insignia, a knight's helmet with a bee hive inside it."

"To show a knight who gave up arms for prayer," said Rosaleen. No statues stood in the garden where she lived, but knowing the insignia was part of a proper princess's upbringing.

Liam nodded. "And, well, bees came and nested behind it."

Rosaleen laughed as falling pink petals blew by.

#

"We must brush the hair perfectly first," said Molly. "Once we start to arrange it, it will be too late. More brushing will disturb the flowers and ribbons."

Rosaleen stood still. With the full, blue skirts about her, she scarcely dared look at Ellen to see if she were rebuked.

Molly muttered about unruly locks as if they intended personal offense to her, but only minutes later turned the other women loose on her hair. And then (Rosaleen swallowed), they opened the door and she proceed out, toward the church, with the women in attendance, and crowds lining the way.

Just the point at which a wicked sorcerer or evil dragon might swoop in to seize the bride and carry her off.

She raised her head and walked with it held high.

The crowd pressed hard to either side of her path, to see the queen, the bride, and held up their small children to look as she reached the church steps. There, Liam's gold hair glinted in the sunlight, and all the crowd cheered, throwing flowers, and ribbons, and caps, in the air.

She climbed the stairs with deliberate speed. Regal and queenly, even. In this gown, it was only prudent. She could not slow the hammering of her heart.

#

After the mass, they returned down the streets to still louder cheers, through the garden which snowdrops and crocuses filled with a new white, and into the royal great hall.

She and Liam received the seats of honor, but to her surprise, the bear did not sit down beside them.

Servants brought out the dishes as if expecting that, and the feast was filled with meat and wine, the new green sprouts, sweets, and finely spiced foods, and abruptly the doors flew open.

A dwarf stood in the middle, his attire rich violet and gold. "A great curse has broken!"

Rosaleen swallowed and glanced about. Liam blinked. Other guests openly gawked, except the dwarfs. Molly lifted her glass in a toast, and the other dwarfs followed. Rosaleen managed to reach for hers, and moments later, Liam did the same.

"Your mothers and even your aged grandmothers could not tell you this tale," said the dwarf, "for it was long before their grandmothers could tell them."

"But know," said Ned, "that it is good that a curse is broken!"

They lifted their cups and toasted the breaking of a curse.

"Once upon a time, not an hour ago," said the dwarf merrily, "I was a bear, because once upon a time, lo these many years ago, a curse laid upon me when the princess of this kingdom escaped to the south, and married the king there. The rest of the royal house perished without an heir. The only claim to the throne that is not spurious would be of her grandson's grandson, King Stefan. Father of Prince Liam."

He turned his face toward Liam.

"As your father's son, we ask you to bear news of his kingdom to him. We have no wish for spurious claimants, or armies to invade."

Part VIII

"You must certainly bring attendants with you, Your Majesty," said the bear-dwarf heartily. "Maidens accustomed to serve ladies. Your husband will not always be beside you, and you need attendants."

Rosaleen, in the great hall, hesitated.

Then she saw a company of seven dwarfs coming toward her. All that she needed to explain. . . .

Then all four of men bowed deeply, and the three women curtsied.

"We can only agree with our greathearted host," said Adam. "It has greatly delighted us to see you thus far, and safely with your bridegroom, but alas, the hour has come for us to part."

Rosaleen looked from dwarf to dwarf. With the bear-dwarf, who had not given her his name, among them. She wondered if the seven names she had learned had anything to do with the other dwarfs.

"Of a certainty," she said, as warmly as she could manage, "I have no reason to complain of your service, or grounds to constrain you. Indeed, I owe you gratitude for your service when others fled."

She hoped it hid her sinking feeling at the knowledge that their aid had brought her this far, and she would have to fare without it after.

She was, after all, a queen.

#

The day of departure dawned cloudy. A soft, dove-gray sort of cloud, Rosaleen noted, but the guides already talked about which paths were safely high, to avoid the spring floods.

Liam's hair gleamed as he spoke with the grooms, and she smiled. He turned and led two horses toward her. She accepted Liam's help in mounting, and was glad the distance required a gentle horse as he mounted his own steed, and they were off, with their news.

And their company. She had not realized before that it was just as well that they went south first, where they did not need her to summon her army.

Then she snorted.

"Is something wrong?" said Liam.

She said, "I thought that it was better to go to your father's kingdom without my army, and so without summoning it, which I would have to do to reclaim my kingdom. But, if we did, we could not bring the army with us to speak with your father. To reclaim my kingdom by force would mean leaving the army there to hold it still against King Henry's forces."

Liam's voice was deep. "We would not leave until we held the kingdom against all comers. It would be our duty."

"Soldiers would discourage many of them, to keep them from attacking at all."

Liam frowned. "True enough."

"But," said Rosaleen, "that would take too long. Your father is old."

Birdsong filled the air from the trees barely showing the first buds of leaves. On the forest floor, spring flowers spread out a green carpet starred with yellow and white. The clouds thinned, and sunlight shone on their way.

#

The crowds gathered far more quickly than when first she reached this kingdom.

With the scattered villages, and the many paths, the crowds could not throng in all the ways, but villagers came and stared all the same. Some cheered when they saw Liam. Some even cheered for her as well. Twice, little girls brought them nosegays of wildflowers.

"I wonder how quickly the message will reach my father," said Liam as they came clopping up to a bridge. "He does have excellent messengers, and any noble would find a company of soldiers reason enough to send a message."

Rosaleen nodded.

"But we, of course, must make haste to the city without stopping."

Rosaleen sighed. Not two months married and they could not stop to coo over each other. Only ride hard and rest for weariness. Even at the city, they had to face his father and the court.

Then her own kingdom, and perhaps war.

Liam reached out and snagged her hand.

#

The capital came into view. Rosaleen swallowed. It swarmed with people, who poured into it as they poured into the village for a festival. Except that all the people in the largest village festival would not have filled one of those roads.

"Do you have the horn ready?" said Liam gravely.

Rosaleen nodded.

No soldiers moved toward them though, and they rode on.

"They are putting up banners and garlands," said Liam softly, as if he did not quite believe it. "Running from one building to the next."

"Yes, they are," said Rosaleen.

"I think," said Liam, delicately, "that we are more likely to feast on meat than fast on bread and water this night."

She could just barely read the excitement he fought down. His heart would be racing. She nodded, and they rode on. The cheers started as they rode closer. Cheers for the prince, and for his lovely bride.

Then, at the city gates, not even the castle's, the king himself awaited them, with his courtiers.

How the crowd yelled and hollered and cheered as Liam dismounted, and the king embraced him, and asked him to present his bride to him.

Feeling strange, Rosaleen accepted Liam's handing her down and leading her, in her travel-stained drab gown, to his father.

He did recognize her.

#

The king's maidservants spared no efforts to make her splendid. They twittered the whole time. How Kevin had broken his neck, fleeing head-long. How Ewan had taken ship with his broken leg before anyone had realized he was hale enough to get that far.

"Prudent," said one woman. "As distant as possible." And then all of them laughed over whether Ewan could find a refuge, whether he could win a princess when he could not work as a gardener's boy, until the smell of food wafted in.

"The cooks are all slaving away," said another. "You'd think they'd have gotten something done in the hours from dawn."

"But," said the chief maidservant, "it's in honor of the wedding! It could hardly be less splendid that for a coronation."

"And has to be better than for a birth," said another maid. "After all, no telling which prince or princess will inherit."

The hum outside the window and inside the corridors increased. Amazing how many arrived so swiftly.

"I see that you got the word out," said Rosaleen.

"Oh, people have talked of it since the prince vanished," said a maid. "And word drifted down from the mountains."

#

The banqueting hall gleamed. If the windows were not enough to light it up, every guest wore gold or jewels, and the table was set with silver and crystal.

She rather gleamed herself, Rosaleen reminded herself. The maids had a reason to deck her in brocade, with sapphires and silver.

Liam, solemn as a judge, gleamed beside her, his arm beneath her hand, and did not hesitate, making her procession easier. The two highest seats at the table stood empty. Rosaleen swallowed. She knew that a king gave way to a bridal procession for peasants, but it felt odd to see it for herself.

Cups rose in toasts to them, and cheers resounded, all the way to their seats. King Stefan smiled and nodded to them. Liam handed her to her seat, and the cheers redoubled, and settled only when the trumpets flourished.

"We could hardly give a queen less than a royal welcome," said the king.

"I am grateful for the guidance," said Rosaleen. "Since I left my father's castle before I remembered anything of it, and the duties of courtesy in a royal court."

His father hesitated, but Liam chuckled. "The cooks would not believe that. They would still worry that you had had better at your father's table."

At which the wine was borne in, and their cups were filled.

"We should enjoy it," she said. "My father's table will not be so grand when it is mine. At least not for some time."

King Stefan raised his eyebrows. "It was for more than the easier roads, and to avoid the snow, that the bear urged you to come here. Already news is spreading that Queen Rosaleen wishes to reclaim her kingdom and her crown. It will spread to your kingdom faster than a crow flies, if things go as they usually do."

"It will not do to be too tardy behind it," said Rosaleen.

#

The cries from the crowd were just as jubilant at seeing them go as seeing them arrive. Then, she thought that they felt no fear. Liam at least was happier, and smiled and waved to the crowd. She smiled herself, but she knew she was only his consort in their eyes.

It seemed to draw some looks. Then maidens began to cheer the prince's bride, the lovely Princess Rosaleen, or the regal Queen Rosaleen, and she had to wave with Liam until her arm was sore, and they rode over a bridge, leaving the cheering crowds behind for pastures with indifferent sheep grazing.

She lowered her arm with relief.

"At least we ride to the woods," said Liam. "The crowds can not gather within. A woodcutter or two at most."

She wriggled her fingers. "I hope the woodcutters have not learned the news of our journey."

He smiled. "They do get news uncommonly quickly, I find."

#

She would have been wiser to wonder whether the news would spread past the forest. Her horse stamped its foot, and she tried to stay calm. King Stefan had hoped too far.

The castle that stood ahead was manned. Her captain sent a messenger ahead to call for them to open the gates for Queen Rosaleen.

"It will look more clever to not admit us," said Liam, his voice low, watching the messenger. "At least, less credulous."

"And then what we will say to persuade?" said Rosaleen. "Or perhaps I will have to summon the army quickly."

"The final argument of kings—and queens," said Liam.

Rosaleen grimaced. "Let us hope we have a fool."

The gates started to open.

"Or a man weary of the war, perhaps," she mused.

To her surprise, the lord came to the gate, and his lady came with him. Indeed, the lady took a step forward, ahead of him. Rosaleen looked at her with narrowed eye.

"Yes," she said, abruptly. "That is indeed the most gracious princess, Queen Rosaleen, who let me and all her other ladies escape from the curse!"

Her hand went to her face, and Rosaleen blinked. The lady actually cried.

The lord came forward, full of welcome, and announced how humbled and gladdened they were to receive their queen. Rosaleen wondered how hard King Henry, and the war, had been.

Liam gravely said they had to discuss claiming the kingdom, stirring still more activity. He, as calmly as if they stopped by an inn, helped Rosaleen down. Her gaze went over the windows, the arched doorway where she could see greenery, and also how the garden door could be sealed. Someone moved within the garden, swiftly along the paths.

"She didn't come for a ball and to dance," called a woman behind the garden wall. "She came to discuss war. She is not expecting great festivities. As long as you do not ask how she came by her soldiers, you will be courteous enough. Besides, she will not be so gullible as to tell you, so there would be no point."

The gate to the garden opened. A woman of middle years, her blond hair turning silver, came out and curtsied. "Your Majesty, the garden is lovely while you wait. The roses are blooming." She lowered her voice. "It would be a courtesy to my uncle, Lord Graycastle. The war has left the land poor, and he has had few guests for many a year."

Rosaleen inclined her head, hoping it was graciously, and accepted Liam's arm.

The roses were indeed lovely.

#

Tongues wagged by the next day, and one of the things they spoke of was how the news spread. The crowds had swollen even in the gray morning, and the lord assured her that people must be coming as soon as the news reached them.

He looked rather gray as he said it.

Liam courteously spoke of how they needed to hunt down King Henry with all haste, all the more in that the reports had him in the south. The lord's expression eased, and he hastened to aid them, and their soldiers, and all the young men.

They rode forth. They were not yet in the lowlands. All about mountains were covered with trees, and the fields and pastures were breaks in them. Yet they saw so many people.

Young men on the way turned on their journeys and joined the throng. Some, from the chatter, had been about other concerns when they realized what lay before them.

Her captain spoke sharply with them. Many reported what lay in the lands about. Some, in answer to orders, bobbed their heads and hurried off ahead and about, scouting.

"Perhaps it will frighten King Henry, the prospect of joining battle," she said to Liam, about noon.

"It would frighten a wise king," said Liam, and she winced.

In the afternoon, her captain came to them both and spoke of the throng that followed.

"The men are not well-off, they are neither well fed nor well armed. They might make good scouts, though."

Rosaleen drew a deep breath. "It would be best for you to have more soldiers, would it not?"

"Indeed," said the captain. "All the more in that these men have not been trained to obey, and that loses more battles than any other flaw."

"We must wait to summon more soldiers. Because of the want of rations."

The captain inclined his head. "All the more with these subjects of yours, who also need rations."

Rosaleen swallowed. "But it is better to summon them too soon than too late. Choose the hour wisely."

"The land, too," said Liam. "Best to summon them in a place to defend."

"The men are of more aid there, sir. They know where fortresses are, and what forces they hold, and who their lords are."

"Let us hope the fortresses all know their rightful queen," said Rosaleen.

Liam stirred, and said nothing. She let her breath out. He did know it was lunacy to even hope that every subject of hers would return to her allegiance at once, and they had to gauge the chance of treachery.

"They'd be fools," said the captain. "When a princess rises from an enchanted sleep to claim her throne, and returns with a prince from a far-off land, they should know she has powerful enchantments to help her."

"King Henry has already shown himself foolishly arrogant," said Rosaleen. "And I have no marvel that will make shelter for even such men as we have. Wisest to look for a wise place to fight from, even if we must make shift for defense."

"It is well that we have scouts, then," said the captain.

#

The first thing a soldier assured her of, in the morning mist, was that scouts had crisscrossed all the ways about them, keeping watch for King Henry's forces.

She walked through the camp, to find Liam and her captain earnestly discussing the news that King Henry was in the south, and how they wished they had news of how close he was.

"Captain, captain!" came a hoarse voice, and a soldier was running toward them. He sketched a bow toward Rosaleen. "Henry's men, they're coming, there's hundreds—"

The captain already looked about as he questioned the man, and began shouting to move the men toward a hill.

Rosaleen said, "Is this the time for an army?"

The captain stopped.

"First we get into place," said Liam. "Then we add the army." His eyes narrowed. "King Henry must have been very near."

"Perhaps a fairy told him," said Rosaleen. A cold breeze pulled at her skirt. "Or both."

"We can hope his men are weary," said the captain, "but we can not rely on it."

#

Sunlight burned mists away. The soldiers of King Henry tramped forward. They filled the green valley with brilliant reds and golds, and the cold gray of steel. Rosaleen glanced sideways. Lady Gilliane had ensured she could tell that their position was the stronger, but still she waited for the captain and Liam to call to fill out their numbers.

She reminded herself that the surprise would help in the fight. The moments still inched by.

Liam appeared by her shoulder like a traveler looming from mists. "Now," he breathed.

She lifted the horn. The blasts rang out. King Henry's army was startled by the first, looking about at the second, contemptuous at the third, startled at the fourth, and as the fifth sounded, and the hillside filled with soldiers in her blue, terrified. Liam and the captain moved about with orders, and she lowered the horn. The soldiers had appeared in good order, ready to fight.

Liam and her captain—no, general—surveyed them. She drew back. They needed to face the foe, not worry about her safety. Even her hurried withdrawal let her see the wavering in the ranks of King Henry's army.

In a hollow, she stopped, and her soldiers arrayed themselves about her. King Henry himself shouted at his men, and their lines stiffened.

Liam shouted to theirs.

Rosaleen looked away. Her heart hammered, but she could do nothing for the battle unless she blew the horn again.

A roar from her men had her glance up in surprise. King Henry's men had started to flee in panic. She let her breath out. A magical army might terrify, but that did not mean the deaths were over.

#

Sunset gleamed, bloodily, in the sky to the west. To the east, stars appeared. Her army still moved over the valley. Some gathered bodies, and others dug graves. Priests from the nearest villages moved among the wounded, or stood at the burials.

Heaven blessed us, that so few died, thought Rosaleen.

"We did find his body," said the soldier. "The banner and the sword make it clear."

"His men killed him as he tried to stop them?" said Liam.

Such disloyalty, thought Rosaleen. They could have fled whatever he did.

"Yes," said the soldier slowly. "They trampled him."

Rosaleen winced. She tried to keep her voice steady. "Make a coffin. Send it back to his kingdom. With the evidence that it is him. It will limit the war."

Liam raised an eyebrow.

"He never married. He had no son. He also had neither a brother nor an uncle." She sighed. "I wonder how long it will take them to find a cousin."

Silence fell. The general surveyed the soldiers as if already reckoning how to defend the borders with them. A breeze made the grass ripple, and chilled the air.

"Here's to hoping the fleeing soldiers found shelter without much trouble," said Liam grimly. "They can still be a peril. Especially to the farmers."

"I have sent patrols," said the general. "We may have to shelter them ourselves. Those whom we find. At least we have tents for our own."

She heard someone clear his throat behind her.

A scout bowed. "Your Majesties. Nearby, there is a royal castle that you could reach on the morrow if you rose at dawn."

#

When they came over the hill and were able to see the castle, Rosaleen laughed a little.

"Barracks," she said as they rode on. "Those must be barracks."

"And no soldiers moving about them," said Liam. "There will be room enough for yours." He glanced about. "Some of yours."

"The wounded first," said Rosaleen. "Including the prisoners." She sighed. "And then the question of how to be ready to fight whoever succeeds to King Henry's throne, and what to do with the soldiers after."

"And whether we can return the prisoners," said Liam. "At least the fleeing soldiers seemed too frightened to return as brigands."

Neither of them spoke of how they might return as an army. They had sent soldiers to harry any that lingered without surrender, but it was their rejoining that could imperil the land.

#

The soldiers had clerks in their numbers.

Of course, thought Rosaleen. How could an army manage without clerks to record men and weapons, provisions and water, horses and armor?

The men sat at tables outside the barracks, under the castle walls, and their pens moved endlessly as they wrote records of soldiers coming and returning on the patrols against the last of King Henry's forces.

"The horn created them knowing that," said Liam. "Or summoned them, somehow."

"Or farming, or how to dig graves," said Rosaleen.

"Farming?"

"Some are helping the widows and other women at farms about the castle," said Rosaleen. "Perhaps they were rescued from battles where they fell, before they died. But at least it makes it simple to manage, with no war on our border. And no army even gathering."

Liam nodded, but said, "I will not be happy until I hear of their new king."

Rosaleen looked out over the fields. Wind shook the branches of an orchard. Perhaps she would not be, either.

"Your Majesties!" The soldier's voice was hoarse. "Your Majesties!"

Rosaleen whipped around. A man ran toward them. Further down the hill, other soldiers took his horse. She bit her lip.

"Your Majesty! It's the nobles from King Henry's lands! They wish to speak with—" He glanced between her and Liam.

"Out with it, man," said Liam.

"With you, Your Majesty." He bowed to Liam. "Her Majesty is, they said, welcome to attend, but they wish to speak with you."

He straightened a little. Rosaleen blinked.

"With a suitable guard, I trust," said Liam, coldly.

"As many as you wish, they said."

Liam scowled.

"Whenever and wherever you wish."

The wind ruffled the grass, and made the banners snap.

Liam muttered, "It still might be a way to draw off soldiers."

That was true enough, but the first message from the kingdom had to be taken gravely.

"How many soldiers will they bring?" said Rosaleen.

The man turned to her. "No more than are needed in case of bandits, they said."

"In that case," said Liam, his face pale but set, "we shall scout about and ensure they brought no more. If they did, we will deal with treachery."

"And if not," said Rosaleen, "we will meet?"

Liam did not speak for a long minute. Then his shoulders slumped, and he nodded.

#

Liam and Rosaleen had consulted counselors to choose, and the counselors had done well. From the hilltop, Rosaleen could clearly see everything over the scythed and treeless fields, down to the bridge where a small company came toward them. They had plenty of time to observe with the distance.

Rosaleen smoothed out her skirts, though the breezes had barely perturbed them. A queen always had to be regal, even with Liam was too intent on the company to notice her.

"They barely have guards," said Liam, abruptly. Rosaleen glanced over. "I would not trust my safety against bandits in these troubled times without guards."

"More than that, they are dressed as if for court," she said. "And a grand day at court. That is how your father's court dressed to receive you, not on the day I arrived."

Liam scowled. "Perhaps—perhaps their guards are with the tents where they changed."

Rosaleen summoned the scouts, who agreed that the company had been larger before, they must have intentionally left all the guards behind. And that took long enough that the company came within shouting distance.

She straightened. Her general was wary, but the nobles drew up before them, far enough away that they could not strike Liam down before the guards could move. One went to open a bundle, and the guards tensed.

Out of the bundle came a cushion in royal blue, bearing a crown of gold and jewels. Rosaleen blinked, and barely managed to see how Liam stared. All the nobles went down on one knee.

"Your Majesty."

Liam stood as impassive as a statue, but he could not keep the color from draining from his face.

He listened, she listened, in silence, as the nobles recounted how King Henry's great-great-great-great-great-grandaunt had fled the land with her beloved, a prince from another kingdom, which they had learned was the very mountain one where the dwarf had ruled in bear-form—after a later princess had fled south, to marry the king of Liam's land.

"And as your father has disinherited your brothers, we have concluded that we, also, wish you to inherit. All the land will accept our word, that you are the rightful king who will bring us peace and justice."

With that, they bowed their heads and held up the crown. Moments inched by, marked out by her heartbeats.

"A humbling request," said Liam. "And not quite rightful. We shall send word to my father."

\#

The army, the great army, stood arrayed before her, brilliant again after the weary duty of burial. Their ranks filled the grassy valley from one wood to the other.

Rosaleen stood straight. This task she could not delegate, since she had summoned them and could not send them back again.

Her voice rang out clearly enough. "With King Henry's forces perished or in flight, with my husband the heir to the rightful heir, you are to go your separate ways."

This time, the soldiers' not twitching did not seem to be mere obedience.

"You have done well in my service. Raised tents, dug graves, herded beasts. Go and put those skills to work in new places, where the men who perished against King Henry had labored in the land."

Part IX

Banners had filled the streets at dawn. The garlands had descended when the bells rang, to be fresh. Most. Some hastily lowered them now that the royal party was in view.

It would be impolite to notice. Connor shouted with delight and waved his hands in air. Some among the crowd pointed, and she smiled. It was, indeed, a great thing when the heir to the throne thrived and prospered.

"The crowd's as grand as the coronation," she murmured to Liam.

Liam laughed. "See how the children play."

She smiled. A fair number of children were, in fact, playing, but— "So many more children in their arms of their mothers and fathers." She wondered how many of those proud fathers were soldiers summoned by her horn. The men had spread over the kingdom, taking on labor, and so many of them had married the daughters who had to be heiresses, or widows of soldiers.

She had had to hear a number of disputes, as uncles and cousins had made claims. Liam had listened in patience and observed that many of them would be disputing something else if the heiress had not found her husband. Lady Gilliane had warned her, but it still surprised her.

It was telling, even unsettling, how grand and loud the crowd was. She had not known how they had dreaded the prospect of having no heir to the throne. Connor leaned forward, babbling, and showers of petals floated through the air with scents of roses.

Rosaleen watched him with care.

When he yawned for the first time, Rosaleen went to pick him up.

Liam helpfully diverted people as she left. The cool and quiet of the shadow brought to bear how glaring the sun had been, and the din of the crowd. "If your daughter becomes queen," she told Connor, "do not pack her away to the mountains. She will be unused to clamor."

Connor yawned.

She reached their private chambers with Connor before he started to wail in sleepiness. Which would not be becoming.

"And no use in scolding you."

Connor rubbed his eyes.

She still took the moment to move his cradle to the garden niche. An overhang from the chamber, it was still surrounded by roses in full bloom. Connor stopped his fussing to stare at them, until she lay him down in the crib. He yawned as the bees bumbled from pink bloom to pink bloom. And then he slept.

She sat. The sunlight barely crept through the leaves to form bright flecks, here and there. The air grew warm even in the shade. She yawned and leaned back.

A brush on her cheek woke her, and the sunlight had shifted, though not far. Connor still slept.

"It will grow colder soon," said Liam softly. "Though it's almost a pity to take you from the garden. It is as if you were telling the roses, 'Roses, there is no need to bloom, for I am blooming.'"

Also by Mary Catelli

Curses And Wonders
Dragon Slayer
Eyes of the Sorceress
Fever and Snow
Mermaids' Song
Sword and Shadow
The Book of Bone
Witch-Prince Ways
Dragonfire and Time
Enchantments And Dragons
Jewel of the Tiger
Over the Sea, To Me
The Dragon's Cottage
The Maze, the Manor, and the Unicorn
The White Menagerie
A Diabolical Bargain
Madeleine and the Mists
Magic And Secrets
The Lion and the Library
The Princess Goes Into The Forest
The Wolf and the Ward
The Witch-Child and the Scarlet Fleet
Treachery And Spells
Winter's Curse
Crow Curse

Free Passage
Isabelle and the Siren
Journeys And Wizardry
Lifestone
Magic of the Lost God
Never Comment On A Likeness
One Name
The Drunken Mermaids
The Turtle in the Sea of Sand
Were I You
Where There Is Smoke
Through A Mirror, Darkly
The Princess Seeks Her Fortune
Oath Keeper
Queen Shulamith's Ball
Ripening Gold
Sorcery and Kings
The Firemaster and the Flames
The Hall of the Heiress
Spells in Secret
The Other Princess
The Enchanted Princess Wakes

About the Author

Mary Catelli is an avid reader of fantasy, science fiction, history, fairy tales, philosophy, folklore and a lot of other things. (Including the backs of cereal boxes.) Which, in due course, overflowed into writing fantasy (and some science fiction).